"I wanted to ask you something."

Lindsey waited.

He was silent.

"Go ahead," she prodded.

"I was wondering if you would have dinner with me tonight."

Seriously? The guy was wearing a hospital gown and booties and had half his body inside an MRI machine, and he was asking her out? Clearly the relaxation meds she'd given him were working. She hesitated. She wasn't sure of Noah's exact age, but she suspected he was at least four or five years younger than she, and given his chosen career, he wasn't even on her radar of potential men to date. A fighter who put constant stress on his body and mind was not someone she would consider as a life partner—and at thirty-five, she thought maybe it was time to start taking relationships seriously.

"I have to work."

D1444088

Dear Reader,

Who doesn't love a man whose beautiful, compassionate inside matches his gorgeous exterior? In book five of the Brookhollow series, Lindsey Harper is struggling with just that—feelings she has for a man she knows she shouldn't fall in love with.

But Noah Parks makes resisting him so difficult, with his irresistible smile (and abs) and his kind heart. And it doesn't help matters that he simply won't take no for an answer.

Fighting for Keeps is a story I've wanted to write for a long time. A story about two people with two very different ideas about MMA fighting and how a compromise could ever be reached...if it actually could.

Being the fifth book in my Brookhollow series, it was a tough one to write. Having to say goodbye to two characters that I've grown to love as friends to the hero/heroines in these books was heartbreaking, but life is about loss, love, second chances and facing adversity. Through the tragic loss in this story, Lindsey gains her own redemption and happy-ever-after love story.

I hope this story makes you laugh, cry and root for Lindsey and Noah and their chance at love.

xo

Jennifer

HEARTWARMING

Fighting for Keeps

—

Jennifer Snow

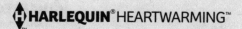

Recycling programs
for this product may
not exist in your area.

ISBN-13: 978-0-373-36723-8

Fighting for Keeps

Printed in U.S.A.

Jennifer Snow lives in Edmonton, Alberta, with her husband and four-year-old son. She is a member of the Writers Guild of Alberta, the Romance Writers of America, the Canadian Author Association and shewrites.org. She is also a regular blogger on the Harlequin Heartwarming Authors site and is a contributing author to *Mslexia*, *WestWord* magazine and *RWR*. Her 2013 holiday romance, *The Trouble with Mistletoe*, was a finalist in the 2014 Golden Quill contest and the Heart of Denver Aspen Gold contest. More information can be found on her website, jennifersnowauthor.com.

Books by Jennifer Snow

Harlequin Heartwarming

The Trouble with Mistletoe
What a Girl Wants
Falling for Leigh
The Mistletoe Melody

Visit the Author Profile page
at Harlequin.com for more titles.

For all of the step-parents out there who love unconditionally, opening their hearts and their arms to children who need them. Dad (Robert) and Reagan—twice in my life I've been fortunate enough to reap the benefits of such compassion and selflessness, and I can't thank you both enough!

Acknowledgments

Thank you to Stephany Evans, whose happy faces on my manuscripts sometimes look like little squares, but I know what you mean. Thank you to my amazing editor, Victoria Curran, whose insight always makes the book stronger.
A big thank-you to Frontier College, which invited me to host their conference on Youth and the Criminal Justice System—the stories I heard that day inspired a big part of this book. And thanks to MMA athletes everywhere for the entertaining fights and the dedication you put into your careers.

PROLOGUE

10 years earlier...not that Lindsay Harper remembers

WHEN LINDSAY TOOK the microphone from Ben Walker, her brother's best man, there was a collective groan throughout the Brookhollow community center, which was elegantly decorated for the event. The wedding guests had already sat through the slightly slurred speech the maid of honor had delivered moments before, filled with embarrassing stories about her kid brother. "Excuse me..." she said into the microphone, tapping it. "Is this thing on?" She laughed as she held the microphone too close to her lips.

"Lindsay, everyone loved your speech... now it's my turn," the best man said.

But she moved the microphone out of his reach and took several steps toward the head table, tripping over the dangling cord as she went in her four-inch heels.

Nathan's smile had faded and his new wife's was forced.

"When my brother told me he was going to propose to Ra...Rachel—" she winked at her "—I was jealous."

Leave it to Lindsay to make her brother's special day about her in some way. It wasn't enough that she'd shortened the maid-of-honor dress to way above the knee—and whether or not she was wearing underwear was still a debate among the table of single men in the corner of the room—or that she'd been ten minutes late to the ceremony and was now questionably sober at that early hour.

Unfortunately it didn't seem as if there was any stopping the train wreck about to happen.

"I mean, he *is* two years younger than me," she continued. "Aren't I supposed to get married first? After all, I am older."

Yes, she'd mentioned that.

"Lindsay, I think we need to move this along," said Jim Bishop, the master of ceremony, reaching for the microphone.

"Stop it," she said, smacking his hand away. She moved closer to the head table. "But then it all made sense—why this we… wedding was ha…happening so quickly."

Rachel's eyes widened and Nathan shot his new bride a questioning look.

Lindsay turned and pointed at Rachel. "I mean, Rachel wanted to look skinny in her wedding photos…and a baby bump sure wouldn't have worked in that dress, would it, Rach?" She smiled at her new sister-in-law.

Nathan's mouth gaped. Both the groom and the bride's mothers turned to glare at each other. Clearly neither had known. Rachel slumped in her chair, her cheeks glowing.

"You're pregnant?" Nathan asked her.

Rachel couldn't look up at her husband.

You could've heard a pin drop in the community center as everyone strained to hear what she would say.

"I was going to tell you later tonight… and everyone else at a later time, but…yes, I am," she said, her voice barely a whisper. She twisted her napkin in her fingers.

"Are you serious?" he asked, cupping his wife's face.

The two sat there, frozen, staring into each other's eyes. All the wedding guests leaned in, trying to decipher the moment.

And then Nathan kissed her, whispered something in her ear, and the pair burst into laughter.

The room erupted into applause as congratulations rang out and more champagne was opened in celebration.

The couple shared another kiss and the mothers-in-law hugged, despite it being no secret they weren't fond of each other, and then went to hug the bride.

Lindsay leaned across the table to join the group hug, but her mother blocked her, so she stood, looking bored and annoyed.

Damage done and no longer in the spotlight, she brought the microphone to her lips again, though no one was really paying attention anymore.

"You're welcome," she said, raising her wineglass to the couple before passing out in a heap on the floor—and settling the bet in the corner.

CHAPTER ONE

"I DON'T THINK this is necessary," Noah Parks said, his eyes wide as he stared at the needle in her hand.

Tough guy was afraid of a needle. What a surprise, Lindsay thought, reaching for his arm. "Well, we do. The last time I slid you in the MRI without the sedative you almost broke the scanner, trying to get out."

"The noise freaked me out," he mumbled, shoving up the sleeve of the green hospital gown to allow her access to his arm.

And what an arm it was. At six feet and two hundred pounds of solid muscle, Noah was the definition of chiseled strength and athleticism.

Even though she was a professional—the head nurse of the clinic—Lindsay wasn't oblivious to the effect his smooth, tanned biceps could have on a woman.

It was too bad he used that strength to

beat the crap out of other men… That kind of ruined it for her.

She cleared her throat as she wiped the injection site with an alcohol swab. "That's why we give you headphones." The scan was painless but without the noise-canceling headphones, patients were often discomfited by the constant thumping and tapping.

She wrapped a rubber tourniquet around his arm and tapped his skin. A quick look at his expression revealed he was already nauseous. "I haven't even poked you yet."

He flinched and gripped the edge of the exam table a second later as the needle pierced the skin.

She shook her head. "You get punched in the face for a living and a tiny prick of a needle makes you woozy." She steadied him. "I'll leave the room for a moment to let you get settled. When you are ready, lie on the table, head pointed toward the machine—" She stopped. "You probably know the routine better than I do by now. I'll knock before I come in."

Picking up his medical file, she left the room and stood outside the door. Scanning his history, she sighed. Three MRIs this year so far. Luckily the magnetic resonance machines didn't involve X-radiation, otherwise the frequency of these brain and tissue scans could be more detrimental than they were worth.

She didn't understand why mixed-martial-arts fighters insisted on a career path that made it necessary to have their brains checked for signs of trauma before each fight. The clinic often saw fighters training at Extreme Athletics for their prefight medical clearance, but none as often as Noah. Three fights since January—what was the guy thinking?

She didn't follow MMA, but even *she* knew three fights in six months were too frequent to be safe.

A glance toward the reception area revealed it was full. And she had to waste a half an hour of her time and everyone else's on this scan. She shook her head as she placed Noah's file on her desk.

Every day she cared for patients with injuries and diseases beyond their control. Patients who would love to be healthy and free of their medical issues.

And then there were guys like Noah—perfectly healthy guys who put their bodies in danger every time they went to work. She'd never understand the sport or the mentality of the men who competed in it.

Tapping once on the door, she let herself back into the room. In most city clinics, a technician performed the scans, but here in Brookhollow, the five nurses on staff had been trained to perform a variety of duties—operating the MRI machine was one of them.

"How do you feel?" she asked Noah. The sedative worked quickly in most cases, but with his body mass, she wanted to be sure of its effect.

"Fantastic."

"Okay." She handed him the headphones. "Put these on and relax. Remember to stay as still as possible. If you move, the pictures will blur and this will take longer." She handed him the communication button. "If you need to talk to me, hit the button."

When he nodded his understanding, she

turned her attention to the controls on the side of the machine. She placed the helmet-shaped scanner over his head and he flashed a wide smile.

"You don't like me much, do you?"

"I'd like you better if you stayed still." She readjusted the metal frame over his ears, checking to make sure his head was centered. His last couple of scans had been clear, but anything could have changed since his last fight.

At least the fighting commissioners took proper precautions, she'd give them that much.

"But you don't approve of what I do."

"I don't approve of any activity that routinely requires a brain scan. Now, *shh*, and stay still." She hit the button on the side and the table slid into the tubular machine even further. She noticed his grip tighten on the communication button. "You okay?"

"Perfect," he said, but his voice was strained.

"Okay, I'll be in the other room, press the button if you need me."

In the lab, she sat at the computer as the scanner performed the first series of scans.

Images appeared on the screen in front of her and, to her experienced relief, nothing seemed to be a cause for concern on immediate viewing. Of course the radiologist and the doctor would review the images in more detail that afternoon.

His communicator beeped and she hit the intercom button. "Noah? Something wrong?"

"No, I wanted to ask you something."

She waited.

He was silent.

"Go ahead."

"I was wondering if you'd have dinner with me tonight."

Seriously? The guy was wearing a hospital gown and booties, had half his body in an MRI machine, and he was asking her out? Clearly the relaxation meds she'd given him were working.

She hesitated. She wasn't sure of his exact age but she suspected he was at least four or five years younger than she was and, given his chosen career, he wasn't even on her radar of potential men to date. A fighter who put constant stress on his body and mind was not someone she would consider as a life partner, even though at thirty-five, she thought maybe it was time to start taking relationships seriously.

"I have to work."

"Tomorrow night?"

"No."

"Oh, come on. You were totally flirting with me at Bailey and Ethan's wedding last weekend."

She cringed. She'd known dancing with him had been a mistake, but when the roster of single men in town was made up of high school boys and the over-fifty divorced crowd, her options had been slim.

It had nothing at all to do with the fact that dressed in a suit and tie, Noah had been the hottest man in the room and his occupation had momentarily escaped her mind.

"I also danced with Mr. Grainger, the seventy-year-old manager of the bait-and-tackle store. Don't read too much into it."

"I'd like to think I was the better dancer at least."

"'Bye, Noah."

A moment later the intercom beeped again.

She hit the intercom. "Maybe I should have specified—unless you're in pain or experiencing anxiety, you don't need to hit the button."

"Wait. I am in pain."

Her eyes narrowed. "Why? What's wrong?"

"I'm heartbroken."

Leaving the room, she walked into the scan area and took the communication device from him.

"Hey, what if I need you?"

"You won't."

OPENING THE DOOR to Victoria and Rachel's B and B later that afternoon, Lindsay ushered Melissa inside, handing her niece her backpack. Several guests lounged in the sitting area and she waved as she scanned the room for her brother. His truck had been parked in the family's designated parking space, which she hadn't been expecting.

"I thought your dad was in Newark this week?" she asked Melissa.

"He got back this morning," the girl grumbled, obviously not pleased about it, either.

"What is on my daughter's lips?"

Ah, there he was.

Aunt and niece rolled their eyes in unison. "The shade is called Pretty in Pink," Lindsay said.

"Tell me you did not have that on at school." The frown lines on her brother's forehead were so deep, he looked like the older sibling…by a lot…she liked to think.

Melissa sighed. "No, Dad. Aunt Lindsay let me try it on in the Jeep on the way home." Lindsay watched as the girl hid the lipstick she'd given her—last season's shade—in her back pocket.

"Well, go wash it off and start your homework," Nathan said.

"Aunt Lindsay wants to watch the episode of *Gossip Girl* we recorded last night," Melissa protested.

"Well, Aunt Lindsay can watch it. *You* have homework first. Besides, I need to talk to your aunt…" His voice trailed as his cell phone rang in his pocket and, reaching for it, he frowned. Again. "I have to grab this. Don't go anywhere," he told Lindsay.

"Where's Rachel?"

"Upstairs bathing the two of my daughters you haven't corrupted yet." Answering the phone, he turned away from her. "Hello? Nathan Harper here…"

Saved by one of her brother's demanding clients. Maybe it was Ben Walker, the friend who'd co-founded the land development firm with him. Lindsay's most recently failed setup. Apparently, according to Ben, they'd met years ago at Nathan and Rachel's wedding. She had no recollection of it.

Bending to whisper in Melissa's ear, she said, "I'll hide from your dad in your bedroom after I talk to your mom. Hurry, so we can watch the show."

Thursday nights were Aunt and Niece Night, but the night before she'd been stuck at work. She hated disappointing the kid. The oldest of five, Melissa was expected to help out, stay out of trouble and, naturally, received the least amount of attention. Lindsay could relate.

"Okay, remember—no smoking."

Seriously, the girl was worse than her own conscience. As a nurse, she knew the habit was a bad one, she knew the health risks, she also knew how terrible it looked to the patients when they caught her outside the clinic doing exactly what she preached to them not to do. The truth was, she'd tried many times over the years to quit and she'd failed miserably every time.

But how could she not attempt it for the fifty-eighth time when her niece had tearfully asked her to stop the month before when they'd watched a video in school about lung cancer?

She lifted the sleeve of her uniform to reveal several nicotine patches. "I'm trying," she told her. And she was. So far she'd only caved twice in a month.

"I think you only need one," Melissa said.

"Well, it can't hurt. Go do your homework," she said, the urge for a cigarette stronger now that they'd been talking about it.

The kid rushed off to do her homework at one of the dining room tables and Lindsay headed upstairs.

In the bathroom of the B and B's living quarters, Rachel was perched over the bathtub. The eighteen-month-old twin girls, Mackenzie and Abigail, splashed in the bubbles while Rachel tried to wash their dark hair.

"What's got my brother out of sorts now?" Best to get a heads-up from Rachel—the rational one of the pair—before dealing with her uptight sibling.

"The Facebook profile you created for Melissa." She didn't exactly sound pleased herself.

The girl wasn't supposed to have told her parents Lindsay'd set up an account for her. Besides, she wasn't stupid, she'd restricted the security settings. "What's the point of being the cool aunt if she's going to rat me out?"

Rachel rinsed the twins' hair. "She didn't. We got a call from Isabelle Thompson's parents. Apparently, Isabelle was complaining that Mel was allowed to have Facebook and she wasn't."

"Wow, do all parents get up in each other's business like that?"

Rachel shot her a look. "Nathan deleted her account."

"Well, at least she won't be upset with me."

"Spoken like a true aunt," Rachel said

with a laugh. "Someday when you have kids, you'll realize if they're not mad at you, you're probably not doing the job right."

"I'm thirty-five and Mr. Right is nowhere in sight...I'm not exactly rushing out to buy parenting books."

"Which reminds me, what happened on your date with Ben? He told Nathan you faked an emergency call halfway through dinner." She frowned.

Great. He'd seen through the lie. She hadn't thought he was paying attention long enough, answering his cell phone twice and replying to several "important" client emails. She'd seen her brother act that way on so many family dinners—and she wasn't sure how Rachel put up with it.

If a man couldn't put work aside for an hour, then she wasn't interested.

"I'm sure he didn't mind. We weren't exactly hitting it off."

"Really? He said he liked you and hoped you could try again sometime."

Not likely. The man was nice and charming and good-looking but there hadn't been a spark between them. He was too much like her brother…probably why they worked so well together, and exactly why he didn't work romantically for her. Her brother was too serious and often far too stressed.

She took life one challenge at a time. The fact that Ben wanted to see her again was surprising but not going to happen. "I wasn't feeling a connection."

"Maybe you need to lower your standards a little. Your one-strike-you're-out philosophy doesn't really give the guys a fair chance, Linds."

Lower her standards? "That's not exactly easy, surrounded by perfect, disgusting couples all the time."

Rachel laughed.

Lindsay sighed as she sat on the edge of the bathtub and lifted Mackenzie from the water, wrapping her in a ladybug towel.

The little girl shivered and she hugged her, wiping the soap bubbles off her legs and feet. Mac giggled and wiggled in her arms.

"'Perfect, disgusting couples'?"

"Yes. You and my brother are the best example of the kind of nausea-inducing love hitting me in the face whenever I turn around."

Rachel and Nathan had been high school sweethearts, which was status quo in the small town, and the couple had five adorable children. As co-owners of the Brookhollow Inn, they were family focused and as solid as any couple could be.

Lindsay had yet to find true love or anything close. Most of her short-lived relationships lasted a month at best. She couldn't find someone who made her laugh, made her weak in the knees and wasn't in too much of a rush to settle down. She wasn't sure how she felt about marriage and kids. Most days, being cool Aunt Lindsay was enough.

"Well, we'll try not to love each other so much," Rachel said, wrapping Abigail in her butterfly towel and letting the water out of the bathtub.

"Rachel, you up there?"

Lindsay winced. Victoria Mason. Another blissfully happily married woman—one who was eight and a half months pregnant.

"In the twins' room," Rachel answered, as

they carried the girls into the bright purple-and-pink bedroom they shared.

A long time passed before Victoria appeared in the doorway, out of breath. "Hi, Lindsay."

"Hey, Vic," Lindsay mumbled, fighting a sense of irritation at the sight of Rachel's partner in the inn. It wasn't that she didn't like Victoria. The opposite was true—she admired and respected the woman who'd left Brookhollow years before to pursue a career in New York City. Lindsay just wished she'd stayed there instead of returning to marry Luke Dawson. A man Lindsay had always had feelings for. Unreciprocated feelings, but still...

"I wanted to say good-night. I'm heading out. The front entrance is locked and no other guests are scheduled to check in tonight."

"Okay, as soon as I put the girls to bed, I'll go down and get the tables set for tomorrow's breakfast," Rachel said.

"It's done."

"Wow, I don't know how you're not dead on your feet. When I was pregnant, I got exhausted walking to the bathroom." Rachel slid Abigail's tiny arms into the one-piece pajamas covered in dinosaurs.

Her frugal sister-in-law reused as much of her older children's clothes on the smaller ones as she could. Nathan's company had picked up in the past year, but Lindsay knew that being self-employed often gave the couple concern, especially with the possibility of five college tuitions to pay for someday.

"Ah, staying busy helps to keep my mind off things." Victoria shrugged, but Lindsay noticed the dark circles under the blonde's tired eyes.

The nurse in her took over.

"Keeping busy is fine, but you really should start taking it easier in these last few weeks. You're going to need your strength for the delivery," she said bluntly. Victoria's blood pressure had been high at her appointment the month before. She was afraid the high-strung workaholic was overdoing it.

Besides running the B and B, the woman was still volunteering on the New Jersey Tourism Board, against her doctor's recommendations. And Lindsay knew the mom-to-be was putting the baby's nursery together, instead of waiting for Luke.

"See? Nurse's orders to take it easy," Rachel said, zipping Mackenzie's fire-truck-printed one-piece.

Victoria held her hands up in defeat. "Okay, okay. I promise to slow down." She kissed both little girls before turning with a wave and wobbling back down the stairs.

When she was out of earshot, Rachel whispered, "I'm worried about her." Her sister-in-law hesitated. "She made me promise not to say anything…"

Lindsay crossed her heart. "Look, I know I'm the source of most of the gossip in town, but I'll consider this patient confidentiality. What is it?"

"She passed out in the kitchen yesterday." Setting Mackenzie in the crib, Rachel pulled the fleece blanket over her and kissed her cheek.

"Had she eaten anything?"

"Yeah, we'd just finished lunch."

That was worrisome. "Okay, thanks for letting me know." Victoria certainly wouldn't have. "I'll make a note on her file to check her blood sugar on next week's visit."

"Thanks, Lindsay." Rachel looked relieved as she turned off the bedroom light and softly closed the door behind them. "With Luke out of town a lot, I worry about her."

"I'll keep an eye on her," she said with a sigh.

When she'd bought the house next door to Luke almost two years before, she'd hoped their "new neighbor" status would bring them closer together, but then Victoria had moved back to Brookhollow.

Living next door to the couple was tough.

Over the past few months Lindsay had contemplated selling her home and moving closer to the medical clinic. Especially now that there would be a family in the house next door.

Maybe being in a less "family friendly" neighborhood might make her single status easier to live with.

NOAH PACED THE GYM, listening to the side of the phone conversation he could hear, as his trainer spoke to the New Jersey athletic commissioner. With the number of *uh-huh... okay*'s and *I understand*'s from Brandon, it was impossible to determine whether the MMA fight next month in Newark would be sanctioned or not.

He needed this fight.

With his record 6-0 since he'd started fighting the year before, under the guidance of Brandon Sheppard and his brother, who owned the local MMA club, he only needed another knockout to be considered for the UFC—the biggest MMA organization in the world.

Not to mention, he hadn't had a payday in six weeks, since his last fight in LA, and the money in his bank account was dwindling. His volunteer role at the local fire station had yet to turn into a paid position, which he'd hoped for when he moved to Brookhollow from Beach Haven the year before.

He was starting to wonder if he'd ever achieve his dream of fighting in the Ultimate Fighting Championship.

He tried to push his strained finances

from his mind as he waited for the verdict on his upcoming fight.

"Okay, thank you, sir," Brandon said as he disconnected the call.

"Well?"

"Well what?"

"Am I fighting next month?" His eyes wide, his hands clenched in fists at his sides, Noah waited.

"Yeah, you're fighting next month."

Yes!

He'd watched countless YouTube videos of his opponent's previous bouts and the Bronx native was nothing he couldn't handle. He and Brandon had identified holes in Romeo Rodriguez's ground game as well as a weak right hook. Noah was prepared to dominate the fight by playing into the weak spots.

Brandon opened his desk drawer and pulled out the medical clearance form, giving it to him. "Once you get the results from your MRI, have Dr. McCarthy sign this. You may need additional blood work—she'll let you know."

Noah winced. It wasn't the needle so much

as the idea of blood leaving his body that made him woozy. Ironic, given his choice of career.

The only plus side to more tests was having a valid excuse to see Lindsay Harper again. He'd been flirting with her for months and thought he'd made headway with her at Bailey and Ethan's wedding. But she'd ignored his every attempt to see her since.

"Speaking of the MRI, how many have we sent you for this year?"

Noah shrugged. He'd known this was going to come up at some point. "Three."

Brandon leaned against the counter, the fabric of his old, ratty Extreme Athletics T-shirt straining at his waist. The coach hadn't fought in years and had relaxed his own training in recent months. "Look, most guys aren't fighting so often. After this fight, I need you to take a longer break, okay?"

He couldn't afford a longer break. He was paying a reasonable monthly rate for the apartment above the gym, but he was already late with this month's rent. He nodded. "Okay."

"I mean it. At least three months."

Three months? That couldn't happen. "What about the UFC? I thought once I win this fight next month, we were going to try to get me onto the August 22 fight card."

Twelve weeks away. With a payout for a win in the UFC, he could afford to take a three-month break from fighting, not before.

Brandon hesitated. "I don't know. Why don't we try for the October…maybe even the November fight card? It will give you a break, repair some of the torn muscles from overtraining…"

Noah shook his head. "I'm fine. I'm at the top of my game Brandon…I need this August fight, then I promise to take a break." Unless the UFC wanted him again right away. Then how could he possibly say no?

"Get through this one, okay? Then we'll talk." Brandon tapped him on the shoulder as he led the way to the mat to resume their training.

"Okay," Noah said, knowing with or without his coach's consent he'd be on the UFC's August fight card.

The only thing standing in the way of his UFC debut was Romeo Rodriguez.

CHAPTER TWO

"WHY ARE THE men bowling in the dark?"
Lily Duke asked, sitting across from her in
the booth at the pool hall cum bowling alley
cum movie theater later that evening.

Lindsay squinted in the dim lighting and
turned in her seat. "They're glow bowling,"
she said, suppressing an urge to roll her eyes
as the pool hall's bartender glanced their
way. "Heather's trying to bring a younger
crowd to the weekly bowling leagues."

"Doesn't she know we are the younger
crowd around here?" Lily laughed, sipping
her wine.

"I don't blame her for wanting to liven
this place up. It could use some new blood,
but I think she's fighting a losing battle."

Heather Corbett was a New York City girl
who'd come to Brookhollow the year before for Victoria and Luke's wedding and
had stuck around. She'd taken over the bar

when Melody Myers had left town to pursue a music career. Heather had redecorated the space as best as she could, adding laminated drink menus to the tables and rearranging the pool tables to create a bigger dance floor. She'd somehow gotten the owner to approve the addition of four big flatscreens, which were now blasting the opening theme song of the UFC's pay-per-view.

That, too, was a new addition to the pool hall's offerings. Lindsay shuddered. "I didn't realize the fights were this weekend." It had been bad enough when sports were showed continuously on the big screens.

Lily glanced toward the flatscreen as highlights from previous fights flashed, her face clouding.

"You okay? We don't have to stay…" Lindsay reached for her coat, but Lily waved a hand.

"No, it's fine." She released a deep breath. "Men hitting each other doesn't really bother me…it was one particular guy beating me half to death that I objected to." She tugged on her sleeve to cover the long scars Lindsay knew were on her forearms.

Her stomach turned. She remembered all

too well how badly hurt Lily had been when she'd arrived in Brookhollow.

Her car had run out of gas outside of town and Bailey had brought her to the medical center after picking her up in the tow truck. Frightened and frantic, Lily'd fought against receiving medical care, despite swollen black eyes, a busted lip and gashes on her right side from a knife attack. Damage caused by the husband she'd been fleeing.

One who was now thankfully in jail in Newark.

"You're safe now," she said, repeating what she'd repeated over and over to the scared woman while the doctors at the clinic had treated her wounds.

Lily nodded. "If you had told me a year ago I'd be free of him and living here with my own clothing store and amazing new friends, I never would have believed it."

"Well, believe it." She gave her hand a squeeze. "We're all so happy you decided to stay."

Especially her. Her reputation in town as being a gossip and a busybody was one she didn't refute, but it made making real friends difficult—it always had. Lily didn't seem to mind, accepting her for who she was.

The small bar grew louder as the fights started and while Lindsay refused to watch them, she could appreciate the physiques of the fighters as they disrobed to climb into the ring. Muscle from head to toe. Strong, alpha males were admittedly her thing—she just wished men with bodies like that didn't come with inflated egos and empty minds.

"They are nice to look at, I'll give them that," she said, sipping her cosmo. An image of Noah's sculpted biceps flashed in her mind.

Across the bar, the man himself caught her eye. In a pair of jeans that hugged his thighs and a black T-shirt with the UFC logo on the front, he looked comfortable, confident and relaxed. His easy you-lied-to-me smile made her glance away quickly.

She groaned.

She should have known with the limited choices for a night out in Brookhollow, he'd find out she'd been lying about having to work.

She reached for a menu. "We should eat,"

she said to Lily, scanning it. She could feel Noah's gaze still on her and her cheeks flushed. Why was he staring at her? She shot him a look. He laughed and took a mouthful of his beer, winking at her over the bottle.

Holy hotness.

She shook her head. What a waste. It was a shame really.

"What's wrong?" Lily asked.

She snapped her attention back to her friend. "Nothing. Why?"

"Who were you looking at?" Lily turned in her seat, glancing toward the group of men watching the fights. "Ah...Noah."

Lindsay's eyes narrowed. "What's that supposed to mean?"

"It's just a matter of time before he wears you down, you know."

"I'll have *you* know, he asked me out again today, and again I said no."

She should be praised for her resolve. Since moving to Brookhollow the year before, Noah had asked her out several times and every time he came into the clinic, he asked for her. He was about as subtle as a brick to the forehead.

Lily cocked her head to the side.

"What?"

"I guess I just don't get it."

"Oh, come on. I'd never even consider dating Noah or any of those guys that train over at Extreme Athletics. I mean, sure they are among the hottest men anywhere, but you know how little respect I have for their career. I'm a nurse. I'll never date a fighter."

"Even though the chemistry between the two of you last weekend at Bailey and Ethan's wedding rivaled that of the happy couple?"

Lindsay scoffed. "It was only a dance."

"Four dances and, believe me, all eyes were on the two of you."

She'd known dancing with Noah at the wedding would spark gossip all over town, but she was used to being a topic of conversation and she'd learned over the years that people believed what they wanted to believe. No amount of protest would convince them otherwise, so she'd given up trying.

"According to Nathan, all eyes were on the length of my dress," she said, rolling her eyes. Her brother would find any excuse to criticize her. They'd once been close...but their differences made it difficult to be friends in adulthood. Her brother was a worrier and slightly uptight. He had trouble relaxing and enjoying life. She saw things differently, wanting to enjoy every moment, and short dresses and dancing the night away were a part of that. If her brother didn't like it...too bad.

"Whatever. You have great legs. Why not show them off?"

"Would you have worn it?" She toyed with the stem of her wineglass. The opinions of others rarely mattered to her.

"No!"

"Great, so it *was* a T-shirt pulled down over my hips?"

Lily laughed. "Maybe. But who cares? You looked great in it... You know what? I may borrow it sometime."

Lindsay laughed. "Yeah, right." She couldn't remember ever seeing Lily in a dress or anything that showed any amount of skin. She knew her friend was self-conscious about her scars, but she also suspected her ex-husband's abuse had been more than just physical.

Heather approached the table with a round of drinks. "Compliments of the hottest man I've seen in here...ever," she said, setting the drinks in front of them and nodding toward Noah.

He lifted his beer in greeting across the pool hall. Heather and Lily all but swooned. Lindsay smiled her thanks before placing her empty glass on Heather's tray.

"Okay, so let me get this straight. You'll dance with him, you'll accept his free drinks, but you won't date him."

If she dated every man she'd ever flirted with, she'd have dated every man under forty in New Jersey.

She smiled at her friend. "Exactly."

NOAH PARKED HIS motorcycle in the back parking lot at the community center late the next morning. The enormous space was home to a dozen after-school programs and summer camps throughout the year, and served as a host venue for weddings and holiday parties, as well. It was a staple in the community and the heart of Brookhollow.

As he took off his helmet, the door to the

center opened and a tall, thin, teenage boy came out. "Hey, Dominic," Noah said.

The kid's face lit up. "Hey, Noah. I didn't think you were going to make it today."

Made him grateful he'd climbed his tired butt out of bed. "Of course. Sorry I'm late." He secured his helmet to the bike and stripped out of his leather Rocket jacket in the hot, early June sun.

"When are you going to let me drive your bike?" Dominic asked, his admiring gaze on the Honda Cruiser.

"The day you get your motorcycle license. How did the permit test go?"

Dominic's shoulders sagged. "Not so great."

What a drag. He'd been hoping the boy's third try would be a success. "Don't worry about it. Next time. You got your road rules book here?"

Dominic nodded unenthusiastically.

"Great. We'll work on it again today." Wrapping an arm around the kid's shoulders, he ushered him back inside the community hall.

To his right, a group of volunteers played basketball with some twelve- to fourteen-year-olds and on his left, at the computer stations, members of the Turnaround program were helping an older teen update his résumé.

Since starting the program nine months ago, they had placed eight kids with local jobs. Noah prayed the government funding for the program continued beyond this first term the city had agreed to as a test.

Brookhollow was a quiet, peaceful town, but that didn't mean there was enough work to go around and that nobody had any problems.

Noah had grown up in a small town very much like this. He knew firsthand what it was like to be a kid from a family that never had enough. And to have parents who... well...who didn't know how to cope with raising a child. He swallowed hard, squeezing Dominic's shoulder before dropping his hand.

This program was there for kids who needed the support they weren't getting at home, kids who were deemed troublemakers by school officials and who were never given a chance to move beyond their circumstances.

From inside the office, Joanne was signaling for him. He nodded and turned to Dominic. "Why don't you find a table and get started? I'll be out in a few minutes."

"Okay, but I really think a hands-on approach would help me learn better."

"Nice try, but your road test will be done with a car, not a motorcycle. Not exactly the same thing."

Inside the office, Joanne Kelly greeted him with a warm smile, then an immediate, "Bad news."

"Fantastic, I love starting the day with bad news. Means the day can only get better. Let's hear it."

Picking up a letter from the desk, she handed it to him. "The National Crime Prevention Strategy has denied our application for funding."

"Again? I thought we jumped through all the hoops this time. How can they continue to deny the funding? This program is designed to do exactly what they're hoping to accomplish at a community level—reduce the number of kids in the criminal justice system."

Noah took the letter and scanned it quickly for the reason. "Lack of sufficient regulations on the program." Again.

He tossed the paper onto the desk and sat in the chair across from Joanne. "I don't know what else to do. We have the New Jersey parole officers on board making sure these kids get to the programs three times a week to meet with their mentors…you're on staff now…" He shrugged.

"I'm a volunteer on loan from MENTOR's partnership program. You need full-time staff. A social worker would be a good start…a real teacher to oversee the tutoring…"

"These kids' grades have improved significantly with the help of mentors. And I've tried to get real teachers involved. No one has the extra *time* to give to the program," he said harshly.

Noah saw through the excuses: no one saw the value in the program. How was that even possible? He was convinced they were helping the kids who'd enrolled.

Weren't they?

He shook his head in disgust. Now was not the time to start having doubts. He would just have to find a better way to prove that the community center mentorship helped change lives for the better.

"Hey, I'm not the enemy here," Joanne chided softly. "I'm just trying to explain why the funding keeps getting denied."

He ran a hand over his short hair. "I'm sorry. I just don't get it. Without funding, I can't hire accredited staff, and without them, I can't get funding."

It had been an uphill battle to even get the nine-month trial approved on the program without regular, accredited staff in place, but he'd assured the city official he'd met with that he was working on it. He was. Joanne had been a good start. Of course, she was correct. She was only on loan and volunteering her time; for how long, he didn't know.

Joanne hesitated, twirling a strand of her bright red hair around her finger.

A nervous habit of hers. Great, there was more she wasn't saying. He waited.

"It gets even worse," she said finally.

"So much for my theory of it only getting better," he mumbled.

"The city sent a letter informing us the Turnaround funding would only be extended until the end of the month…they say the program hasn't produced enough significant results to warrant their support beyond that."

"Not enough significant…" Noah stood with his hands on his hips, fighting to control his anger. Joanne was just the messenger. He wouldn't take his frustration out on his only real supporter.

He took a calming breath before saying, "How can they say that taking eight kids off the street isn't significant enough?" One of the eight had even returned to finish high school at nights.

"Because last month, twenty kids in New Jersey were incarcerated. Unfortunately it's a numbers game, Noah. We have to prove the program is working. And now I'm going to say something that will probably make you even more angry, but I'm going to say it anyway."

He waited. What he both appreciated and

hated about the woman was her blunt candidness. He suspected today he was going to hate it.

"You need to be here more. If this program has any hope of success, it needs you. The volunteer mentors are trying, but they need direction and guidance."

He knew she was right. He'd started the program when he'd met Dominic. The boy had been walking home with a bleeding lip and tears in his eyes. After much prying, the boy had told him that the injury was a result of him refusing to participate in a gang initiation break-and-enter at an abandoned warehouse outside town.

Noah's admiration of the boy's courage and strength to do the right thing had sparked a fire in him to help kids like Dominic find alternatives to a criminal path. Kids who wanted to do the right thing but couldn't find a way out of the trouble they were involved in.

Kids like him at sixteen.

In less than a year he'd grown the afterschool mentoring and outreach program to fifteen student volunteers three times a week, each paired with two at-risk youth in the community. The mentors were potential at-risk older teens who'd found purpose and direction in helping younger kids.

The motto of the program was "We are all on the same journey, just at different points."

The common stories shared between mentors and mentees brought them closer and instilled confidence and respect in the younger kids. Noah shared his own story of going down the wrong path with these kids over and over in the hope of being a role model for these children.

The only real problem was that the program was growing at the same time as his fighting career. Something he hadn't fully considered.

As much as he knew how important his direct involvement was to the future success of the program, he couldn't be in more than one place at once and his training was important, too.

"I'll figure something out."

Joanne didn't look convinced as she nodded. "Okay, what do I do in the meantime?"

"Please keep reapplying for the funding. The worst they can do is keep saying no, right?"

When she opened her mouth to respond, he shook his head. "Don't answer that."

He knew that wasn't the worst they could do. In truth, without the proper regulations in place and a permanent on-staff director who could be held responsible for the program, the city could shut it down at any time.

Opening the office door, he joined Dominic at his table.

If nothing else, he was going to help this kid get his driver's license.

LINDSAY ALL BUT ran from one examination room to the other where patients were waiting far too long to see a physician. Some kid had come back from an early summer vacation in France with a bad case of chicken pox and had succeeded in infecting the rest of Brookhollow Elementary with the disease.

Sixteen confirmed cases and counting already that day. Itchy, irritable children were bad, but they were nothing compared to the group of men who'd come in contact with poison ivy on a hunting trip.

People scratching themselves every which way she turned would have been almost funny, if she wasn't so exhausted. Like most medical facilities in small towns, Brookhollow's clinic provided a wide range of services and ran on a skeleton crew. Which was usually okay, until an outbreak occurred. Then the staff was expected to work double shifts and no one came out of days like this in a good mood.

She grabbed the next file from the reception desk.

Great, one of the grumpy men. At least he was the last of that group. "Mike, you can follow me," she said, noticing Noah waiting near the clinic door. The small space was at standing-room capacity. "You here to pick up your results?"

"Yeah." He nodded. "Don't worry, I can wait."

"Thanks. Give me a few minutes," she said as she led Mike to an exam room. "Dr.

McCarthy will be a few minutes. Try not to scratch."

She shut the door and headed down the hall toward the file cabinets. Noah's MRI results had come in that morning. He was all clear to fight, and she wasn't sure why the positive results annoyed her. Of course, she'd never want anything to be seriously wrong with him...or any of her patients, but if only there was enough reason not to provide medical clearance.

Picking up the letter from Dr. McCarthy and a copy of the results to send to the fight committee, she went back to the desk and nodded for Noah to come forward.

"I could have waited."

She shook her head. "We're trying to limit wait times for anyone not here with chicken pox. The last thing we need is an adult outbreak."

The clinic door opened and Victoria waddled in.

Oh, no. "Give me a sec," she told Noah. Rushing toward the front door, she ushered Victoria back outside, reaching for a bottle of hand sanitizer as she went. "No! No! Get out…"

Victoria frowned as they walked into the hot sun. "What are you doing? I have a checkup with Dr. McCarthy today and I have to pee." Her eyes widened as she held her baby bump. "This kid is using my bladder as a trampoline."

"We will have to reschedule and you'll have to pee somewhere else." Lindsay took Victoria's hands and pumped the sanitizer on them. "There's an outbreak of chicken pox in there."

Victoria immediately took several steps away from the clinic, furiously rubbing her hands. "Is it serious?"

"Sixteen cases so far today."

Victoria moved farther away from her.

"I'm fine. Nathan and I had them as kids. Mom sent us to go play with Jonathan Turner when he had them one summer." Lindsay had had to miss Brownie summer camp that year and instead had been stuck in the house all week with Nathan.

She could understand the logic now, but

try explaining it to an eight-year-old who missed summer camp.

"Anyway, let's rebook your appointment for next week…" She paused, remembering what Rachel had said about Victoria passing out. "You know what, I'll stop by your house tomorrow morning and take your blood pressure and some routine tests."

"Since when does the clinic do house calls?" Victoria eyed her suspiciously. "Rachel told you I passed out, huh?"

Okay, her sister-in-law couldn't blame this one on her.

"Yes. She was worried about you."

"Who else knows?"

Lindsay suppressed a sigh. She deserved that. Her reputation around town as the local one-stop-gossip-shop wasn't entirely baseless. She did like to gossip…as long as it didn't hurt anyone. "I filed it under patient confidentiality. Now, go home and rest and I'll see you tomorrow morning, okay?"

"Thanks, Lindsay."

Parked in the visitor space, Luke jumped down from the driver's side of the truck when he saw his wife approach. He frowned, but then waved to Lindsay once Victoria explained the situation to him.

She smiled and watched Luke lift Victoria into the passenger seat.

That should have been her, she couldn't help but think. Oh, well, maybe someday... Well...not someday with Luke, but someday with someone else. Someone better.

Yeah, right, as if that were possible.

Back inside the clinic, she returned her attention to Noah. "Sorry about that."

"What *was* that? I mean, it's no secret Vic's not your favorite person, but kicking her out of the clinic is kind of harsh, don't you think?" He smiled as he leaned against the counter.

Lindsay laughed for the first time that day as she pushed his arms away from the counter. "Seriously, this place is infested, don't touch anything," she said, disinfecting the counter with sanitizer wipes for the millionth time and handing him the sanitizer, which he refused. "And I sent Victoria away because she's pregnant and the virus can harm an unborn child."

"Oh, wow, didn't know that."

She flipped through his paperwork to make sure everything was there. "So, everything came back normal and you're cleared to fight." She'd delivered the good news through clenched teeth.

He took the paperwork. "Why do you disapprove of fighting so much?"

She was sure they'd had this conversation already. "It's pointless and brutal. Two men hitting each other... I guess I don't see how that can be considered a sport."

"There is technique involved," he said. "And a lot of training and conditioning..."

"I'm sure there's more to it than I know." *Or want to know.* She picked up the next file. "As fascinating as I'm sure it is, I have to get back to work."

"What are you doing later?" He blocked her path to the waiting area.

"Working."

"You've used that lie already."

She pointed to the crowded waiting room. "It's hardly a lie." Today.

He grinned. "Okay, so what you're saying is if you didn't have to work tonight, you'd have dinner with me?"

"Not at all. What I'm saying is, if I didn't have to work tonight, I would need to come up with a lie."

"I...JUST...DON'T...GET...IT," Noah panted between punches on the heavy bag an hour later.

On the other side Brandon held the bag as he continued his rain of jabs and strikes on the worn leather. "Look, man, I'd like to help you, but women troubles are not really my thing."

"We haven't even made it to troubles yet, she just straight-out refuses to even have dinner with me because I'm an MMA fighter. It's actually kind of prejudiced." Noah threw one final jab, then hit the mat at his feet in push-up position. "I mean, it's like she assumes fighting is all I am."

"Isn't it?" Brandon asked, adding a stack of weights on his back.

Noah struggled with the last two, his forearms burning after the intense twenty-minute circuit set. "No way."

He wondered what his coach would think if he knew about the outreach program.

Since coming to Brookhollow, he'd made some great friends, Brandon and his brother Jordan included, but he was careful about what he chose to reveal about himself.

The families he'd met in the small town were so different from his own. They were supportive of one another, divorce was rare and his friends... Though they'd had their struggles they had never had to wonder where their next meal would come from or have to help their passed-out father to bed after far too many drinks.

Revealing the good he was trying to do would only spark conversation about the bad in his past. And he'd moved away from that. He wanted his friends to see him as the man he was now.

"I've got other things going on," he said noncommittally as he rolled onto his back and brought his left knee and right elbow together in a crunch.

"The thing is," Brandon admitted, "I'm not getting your attraction to her."

"You're kidding, right?" How could the men in this town be so blind to Lindsay's appeal? She was smart, beautiful, kind...

Impossible to reach. He was no stranger to chasing a pretty woman, but he'd believed her when she'd said she wasn't interested. He just wasn't sure he could accept that answer. Not this time. Not with her.

"Okay, maybe I've pegged her wrong. So enlighten me. What does it for you?"

"For one, she's a knockout." Noah did his twentieth crunch and his stomach started to burn. He loved that feeling, so he pushed on.

"I'll give you that. She's definitely one of the more attractive women in town," Brandon said.

Noah let out a deep breath as the crunches got tougher and his abs hardened.

"And she's educated," he huffed, recalling how Brandon's sister had filled him in on all the details on Lindsay the first night he'd noticed her at Bailey's Thursday-night self-defense class at Extreme Athletics.

"She's amazing with her patients."

"Okay, so, maybe it's a Florence Nightingale syndrome. You get hurt a lot, she has morphine?"

Noah shook his head as he stood. His buddy would never get it. Once opinions and stereotypes were formed in small towns, they were tough to shake. And Lindsay fit a clear stereotype in Brookhollow. He knew firsthand how annoying it was to be pegged a certain way and never given the benefit of a doubt. That was why he kept his past a secret from his friends. "Never mind."

"Okay, maybe I can see why you like her, but, man, she *does not* like you," Brandon said, tugging off Noah's training gloves and unwrapping his hands.

"Believe me, I've noticed."

It only made him want her to even more.

His entire life he'd met with challenges and adversity and he'd been successful in overcoming a lot. Could he meet the challenge of the five-foot-two, brilliant blonde who held firm to her own prejudice about him?

LINDSAY CRINGED AT the sound of the clinic door opening. The fourteen-hour shift continued with no end in sight. Her feet ached, even in her practical nursing shoes, and the last thing she'd eaten was half a protein bar as she'd rushed from one patient to another.

All she wanted was a cigarette, but each

time she reached into her purse for her emergency pack, she heard her niece's teary plea.

This day couldn't end soon enough.

As she turned toward the door she almost wished it *was* another infected six-year-old as her eyes met Noah's. What was he doing here again?

"Noah, if you have another self-inflicted injury—" She stopped when her gaze fell to the picnic basket he carried, the smell of fried chicken from Joey's diner on Main Street filling the tiny waiting room.

Several patients, who'd been waiting hours to see a doctor, stared longingly at the basket and she had to swallow to stop from salivating.

"You brought your dinner into a medical clinic where people have been waiting for hours to see a doctor?" Talk about insensitive.

"It's not for me," he said, moving the magazines aside on the waiting room table. Setting the basket down, he opened it.

Lindsay's eyes narrowed as she watched him remove two large buckets of the chicken and a stack of paper plates and napkins... and Tina's famous potato salad...

Her weakness.

"Everyone, help yourselves," he said, opening a grocery bag and handing out apple juice to the kids.

The waiting, hungry patients didn't need any more prompting as they passed around the plates and the food.

Huh, that was...unexpected. And a little bit fantastic.

He took a smaller container from the basket. "Here. I wasn't sure if greasy, fried food was your thing, so I brought you a BLT, with a side order of potato salad."

Above and beyond. Who would have thought?

"Thank you. This was really nice of you." She hesitated, still a little dumbfounded, but more than a little starving.

"Take a few minutes to eat. They are." He nodded to the group devouring the impromptu food delivery.

"Okay." She headed down the hall, but paused when she noticed he wasn't following her. "You coming?" Her question must have surprised him as his eyebrows shot up.

He smiled. "No, you're busy. I just wanted to stop by to take care of the pretty lady who's taking care of everyone else."

She felt her cheeks go red. "Well, thank you. Again."

"Anytime," he said over his shoulder as he left.

Unwrapping the sandwich where she stood, she watched Noah cross the parking lot to his motorcycle. So dangerous, so carefree—he really was the kind of man who preferred to live life on borrowed time.

She could never be with a man like Noah, but she had to admit, with each delicious bite of her BLT, she was beginning to feel huge regret about it.

CHAPTER THREE

LINDSAY YAWNED AS she shut down her office computer. The children with chicken pox and the men with poison ivy had all been treated and she'd finally been able to lock the walk-in clinic doors. If she couldn't smoke, a glass of wine and a bubble bath were the next best thing waiting for her at home.

She stood and was about to turn off the clinic lights, the last one to leave, when she noticed the half BLT she'd left on the desk four hours ago.

Immediately her thoughts went to Noah. He was trying. But, unfortunately, she didn't see a way around his career. It was too bad, she thought, because there was no denying the spark between them.

Sighing, she tossed the now-soggy sandwich into the trash and pulled the plastic bag out and tied it.

Carrying the bag outside, she tossed it

into the large garbage bin. Then, back inside, she set the alarm.

"All doctors and nurses report to Emergency stat," came the call over the clinic's PA system as the alarm started to beep.

Lindsay groaned. So close…

After disarming the security system, she made her way quickly down the hall toward the elevators. Emergency was on the third floor and after hitting the button, she shook herself awake. Double shifts were not uncommon, though emergency stat orders were.

And there was no questioning the severity of things as the elevator doors opened and she stepped out into the hall. An ambulance stretcher whizzed past her, followed immediately by a second.

Her heart raced. An accident? Outside, she could see the flashing lights of the ambulance and the fire truck, and her mouth went dry. She rushed to the nursing station. "What happened?" she asked Kimberly-Ann, one of the ER nurses on duty.

The woman looked pale as she shook her head.

"Kimberly-Ann!"

A man she didn't recognize, wearing a Brookhollow Police Station jacket, spoke. "There was a collision on Highway 14. A transport truck lost a load of plywood." He paused. "I'm Sherriff Matthews, the new..."

Lindsay didn't care who he was. She shot into motion, heading toward one of the operating rooms where the two doctors on staff were talking to the paramedics.

She was a step away from them when, from behind, an arm wrapped around her waist, preventing her from going farther. She whipped around, freeing herself. Noah, in his firefighter uniform, grabbed her arm, keeping her in place.

"What are you doing?" she demanded.

He swallowed hard, his expression dark. "I don't think you should go in there," he said firmly.

Oh, no. "Why not? Who did they bring in?" Her mouth felt like sandpaper and her knees buckled slightly.

He hesitated.

"Who is it, Noah?" She broke away from him, ready to run to the operating room.

"Nathan and Rachel."

Turning, she made to sprint toward the double doors leading into the first operating room, but Noah's strong arms around her waist lifted her off the ground and moved her away.

"Let me go." Frantically she struggled, but his hold tightened. "I have to get in there… *all* nurses…" This was her job, dammit, and it was her family in there. "Let go!"

"No. You can't keep a straight head in this situation."

"Put me down." She pushed against his arms as Kimberly-Ann stepped in, the new Sherriff beside her.

"Dr. McCarthy said not to let you go in… not yet."

The struggle left her and her body went limp in Noah's arms. It was serious… They weren't okay… They weren't letting her in. That only meant one thing.

She broke out of Noah's grasp, but he stood guard, blocking her access to the hallway.

"How bad are they hurt?" She didn't recognize her own voice as she asked the question.

"Lindsay…"

"How bad!"

His gaze and shoulders dropped simultaneously. "We were first on scene. There was nothing we could do for Nathan."

Her chest tightened and she couldn't catch a breath as the room spun around her. What exactly was he saying?

"Paramedics confirmed time of death when they arrived," he said gently. "I'm so sorry, Lindsay."

"Here…sit," Kimberly-Ann said as she took her arm and they tried to help her to a chair.

She fought them. "What about Rachel? Where are the kids?" Her stomach turned and she swallowed to keep from vomiting.

"The kids weren't in the van."

A sob of relief escaped her and her hand flew to her mouth.

Noah hesitated, casting a glance toward Kimberly-Ann before saying, "Rachel is in critical condition. It doesn't look good…" His hands were rubbing her arms, but she felt nothing.

His voice faded as her mind reeled. Nathan—dead? Rachel—critical? How?

How was it possible that this could happen? She'd seen them two days ago...

The kids... Thank God they hadn't been in the vehicle. She dove for the trash can behind the ER desk, emptying the contents of her stomach.

Noah was bent at her side as she fought to catch her breath. "How...how...what...I need to..."

"Just breathe..." He glanced at Kimberly-Ann. "Is there something we can get her?"

"I need...to...to see Nathan." She stood and tried to move past him. Nathan couldn't be dead. That was ridiculous... He had five children...five *small* children. Another sob escaped her. "I need to go in there..."

Noah wrapped his arms around her tightly and pulled her against him on the floor. "Not yet," he whispered.

She clutched the fabric of his jacket and buried her face in his chest as her tears soaked the front of his shirt. "I need to see him."

He hugged her tighter. "I'm so sorry, Lindsay. There's nothing you can do for him."

LINDSAY CLIMBED THE stairs to the living quarters of the B and B three hours later. The house was silent in the 3:00 a.m. darkness, the only light escaping beneath the bedroom door of the nursery, where she knew the twins' butterfly night-light provided the toddlers a sense of comfort while they slept.

Her eyes were heavy and her legs were cement blocks as she walked down the hallway toward the room that had been Rachel and Nathan's. A room they would no longer sleep in...

Rachel had passed away an hour ago. Her struggle to survive the heavy brain trauma she'd suffered in the accident had been a fight she couldn't win, and her soul had joined her husband's.

Opening the bedroom door, she stepped inside and her legs immediately gave way beneath her.

They were gone. No matter how many times the thought crushed her, she couldn't believe it. She'd witnessed the coming and passing of life so many times as a nurse, but this loss was beyond her comprehension.

They were so young. They were so in love. They had five precious children who needed their parents.

A sob choked her as she lay on the hardwood floor and pulled her knees to her chest. Her shoulders trembled violently as tears pooled on the floor beneath her.

She wanted nothing more than to close her eyes and wake up to find this was all just a nightmare. That her brother and sister-in-law were fine.

But the cold truth remained. In three hours the sun would come up and she would have to tell the children their parents wouldn't be coming home.

THE AIR WAS cool as Noah headed away from the bed-and-breakfast after first driving Lindsay home to collect her things. She hadn't even put up a fight about handing over the keys to her Jeep and allowing him to drive. She'd mumbled, "The B and B," when he'd asked her where she wanted him to take her and then she'd been silent on the short drive there.

Torn between wanting to give her space

and to comfort her, provide a safe place for her to grieve, he'd driven slowly and quietly, leaving her alone with her tumultuous thoughts.

He knew loss. It created a hole that couldn't be filled with kind words or warm hugs. She had to learn how to deal with this her own way, to find her own coping mechanisms to face the days ahead.

Big raindrops started to hit the ground in front of him as he walked. He shivered in the fog. In the distance the town clock bells rang three times. He quickened his pace as he rounded the corner to the street, heading toward the fire hall.

In four hours his shift would be over and he'd head back to the B and B where he intended to be whenever he was needed and not too far from when he wasn't.

Lindsay wouldn't be alone.

LUKE FORCED A steaming cup of tea into Lindsay's trembling hands early the next morning before joining his wife on the sofa across from her in the B and B's living room.

Victoria had yet to speak a word without sobbing, so she sat quietly, numb from shock as tears flowed down her cheeks.

"Try to drink this," Luke said, handing another cup to his wife.

She knew he was as tormented as they were, but Luke had adopted the role no one else could handle that morning. He was being the strong one, doing what needed to be done, including telling the three oldest children. They'd decided to let the babies sleep, unsure how much the toddlers would understand.

With both of Rachel's parents already deceased, and Nathan and Lindsay's parents in Phoenix, the three of them did their best to deal with a situation no one ever wanted to find themselves in.

"It's been an hour and they haven't come out of there," Lindsay whispered, her eyes filling instantly with new tears as she glanced up the stairs to Melissa's room, where the little girl had locked herself and her five-year-old brothers inside. Hopelessness was by far the worst of the emotions competing within her, she decided.

"Give them some time…they are going to need each other through this," Luke said, turning away quickly and covering his eyes.

The sight of his strength finally wavering reduced both women to even more of a mess.

Quickly pulling himself together, Luke cleared his throat and wiped his eyes. "I'll go get the girls," he said, taking the stairs two at a time.

Lindsay set the cup aside and forced several deep breaths.

"I can't believe this is actually happening," Victoria said, her voice sounding far away.

"I know." Nothing about the past eight hours felt real. There was so much to be done, yet she didn't think she had the strength to stand, let alone make funeral arrangements and contact the remaining family and friends.

Luke had also taken care of calling her parents, who'd booked seats on a plane to Newark that day. She supposed she would have to go pick them up.

The front door to the B and B opened,

but neither woman looked up. The idea of a guest arriving to check in hadn't occurred to Lindsay.

Life didn't go on after a tragedy like this, did it?

"Hi," Noah said, walking in. He gave her shoulder a squeeze, but she barely felt it. "I wanted to stop by…see if there was anything I could do."

She cleared her throat and forced her voice not to break as she said, "No, I don't think so." The problem was there was too much to do, too much she didn't want to do…all things she couldn't hand off to anyone else.

"What about your parents?" Victoria said suddenly. "Maybe Noah should go with you to pick them up from the airport."

"I can do that," he said quickly.

"No…it's okay."

"I don't think you should drive," Luke said, coming back downstairs, a toddler in each arm.

At the sight of the smiling, oblivious girls, Lindsay's knees started to shake and she bit back the emotions strangling her.

They would be too young to even remember their parents. Somehow she had to make sure they would know them as they grew up without them.

Another thing she had no idea how to do.

Noah sat next to her and accepted one of the girls from Luke, bouncing her gently on his knee. "It's decided, then. I'll drive you to pick up your parents."

She had no fight in her to argue. Besides, it was probably a good idea. In her trance-like haze, anyone else would be safer behind the wheel.

Their family didn't need another senseless tragedy.

"Damn," Lindsay muttered in the passenger seat of her Jeep as Noah took the exit onto the highway leading toward Newark.

Asking what's wrong seemed like a dumb question that day, as nothing in the world felt right, so he placed a hand on her arm. "It's going to be okay," he said before realizing that didn't sound much better. He had no idea if things were going to be okay. All he did know for sure was that he would be by her side through it all—whatever she needed. "I'm sorry."

"No…um…thank you. I just realized I need to make another call and I left my cell at the B and B."

"Do you know the number? You can borrow mine." He handed it to her.

"It's long distance."

"It's fine. Go ahead…please."

"You sure?" She hesitated before starting to dial.

"Make a hundred if you need to, sweetheart," he said, squeezing her arm, before turning his attention to the road to give her as much so-called privacy as possible.

He was so glad she hadn't insisted on making this drive alone. Her mismatched flip-flops—one pink, one purple—further confirmed the fact she wasn't thinking with a clear mind. How could she be? Her brother and sister-in-law had just died, leaving five small children in her care. At least he'd assumed, as their godparent, she'd be their new legal guardian, as well. A position everyone prayed they never had to step into when they agreed to such an important place in a child's life.

"Hello…Ben," she said a moment later.

Ben? He wasn't sure who that was and he ignored the slight pull of jealousy in his chest.

"Yeah…I had fun the other night, too…" she mumbled, shooting a quick glance at Noah who pretended to be checking signs along the road. "Um, listen. I have to tell you something…about Nathan."

Less than a minute later, after she had haltingly told him the bad news, she sat staring at the phone in her hand. "He hung up."

"What?" Noah took the phone from her and tucked it into his pocket.

"That was Nathan's friend—his business partner—in Newark. He hung up."

"Did he say anything before he did?"

She shook her head.

Noah wasn't an expert on the complexity of human emotions, but he could guess the meaning of this reaction. "He's probably in shock, like the rest of us."

She stared out the window in silence and he longed to pull over and wrap his arms around her. Instead he opened a bottle of water he'd brought along and handed it to her.

She took a sip before speaking. "He's the children's godfather."

"Ben?"

"Yeah. He and Na—my brother went to university together. They started Walker Harper Developments, a property development company, five years ago. I can't believe he hung up like that."

Noah sighed as he reached across and took her hand in his. "Isn't it the reaction we all would have liked to have had?"

She held his hand tight, her gaze still out the window. "I guess so. But, surely, after a moment to digest it, you'd call back?" She let out a deep breath as she leaned her head back against the seat. "I don't think it's even fully sunk in yet, you know?"

Noah nodded. He did. Even seeing the accident site the night before hadn't made it more real.

"I keep expecting to wake up from this horrible nightmare."

He nodded again, feeling useless. He had

no idea what to say or even if she wanted him to say anything.

"We weren't close," she said after a long minute of silence. "We were so different, it was always hard to find common ground. That doesn't mean I didn't love him." Her voice broke and tears gathered in her eyes.

His heart ached for her. Brushing her hair away from her face, he wiped the tears from her cheek. "I'm sure he knew that."

"I'm not," she whispered.

LINDSAY SAT ACROSS from her parents in the sitting area of the B and B the next morning, the bomb they'd dropped on her too much to take so soon after Nathan's death. "Do we really need to discuss this right now?"

"The sooner the better," her mother said calmly.

Her father's gaze hadn't shifted from the gazebo in the backyard and it was hard to tell if he was even listening. He wasn't going to be of any help with her mother, not that he'd ever really stood up for what he'd wanted. Since his stroke the year before, he didn't speak, and today he didn't even seem to be in the same room.

Lindsay took a sip of her coffee. Her hand shaking, she spilled it down the side of the cup. She stood to get a napkin, but her mother caught her by the arm. "Leave it."

She tensed, memories of her mother's temper flashing in her mind. Growing up, they'd walked on eggshells around her, not sure if her ever-changing mood would earn them a hug or a smack.

She sat, feeling like a child again. She'd known having her parents here would only cause her more stress and anguish.

She hadn't expected comfort at this difficult time.

She also hadn't expected their immediate launch into the children's future living situation. "Look, Mom, I really don't know what the best thing—"

"*We* are the best thing," she said, her tone leaving no room for argument.

Lindsay seriously doubted that. How her sixty-year-old mother thought she could raise five children and take care of a husband with failing health was a mystery to her. And that she really thought they were the best choice of guardians over her was another knife to the chest. "The will states—"

Her mother scoffed. "The will is a piece of paper, Lindsay."

She cringed at the way her mother said her name. Lind*say*. Condescending, demeaning, as if she was stupid. Maybe she was, but she could barely think straight enough to get out of bed in the morning, how did her mother expect her to make any decisions right now? Why was it so important to decide anything right now?

"Look at your life. You work long hours and then you go out—everyone knows you like to have fun. You're thirty-five-years old and not a long-term relationship to your credit. Nathan told me about that Facebook account." She tutted.

Her brother's never-ending search for approval from their mother had often extended to using their mutual disdain for her life choices as a common bond.

"That was a mistake."

"There's always a mistake or someone else to blame. You have to start taking responsibility for your actions. And until you do, how do you plan to be a guardian to these kids?" She shook her head. "They'd be better off with Ben."

A large lump gathered at the back of Lindsay's throat. She forced it down. "You mean Nathan's business partner and best friend who hung up on me yesterday and hasn't even called back, let alone arrived?" The funeral was scheduled for the next afternoon.

"No doubt you made him feel unwelcome."

Why did she even bother?

"He's such a wonderful man...I can't imagine what you could have said to make him feel that way."

Enough. She couldn't take any more. Standing, she picked up her coffee cup. "I'm out. I can't have this conversation right now."

"Grow up, Lindsay. You can't keep running away when things get tough." Her mother's voice tore a hole through her as she walked from the room and continued out onto the front deck.

She took a deep breath once the door

closed behind her. A desperate need to run away, and confirm her mother's opinion of her, made her stomach turn. Exhausted, she sat on the front step and set her coffee cup next to her. She'd barely eaten anything in two days and even the coffee was making her feel nauseous. Leaning her head against the railing, she closed her eyes.

Grow up.

How many times over the years had she heard that or something like it from her mother? Yet, when she tried to 'grow up,' it still didn't seem to make her mother happy. Even her decision to go into nursing had provoked her mother's criticism.

"You think you're cut out for nursing?" she'd scoffed at the time, making it clear she didn't.

In fact Lindsay had wanted to be a doctor, but her grades would never have gotten her into med school. She would never have been able to afford the tuition anyway.

"School has never been your strong point, Lindsay. Nathan's the smart one." Her mother had never hidden the fact that she had a favorite child. And after a while,

Lindsay had given up trying to be like her brother.

She wasn't Nathan.

"Aunt Lindsay...you okay?"

Lindsay's eyes flew open at the feel of a tiny hand on her shoulder, her heart racing. "Jacob?"

"Were you asleep?" Jacob asked.

She sat straighter, moving over to make room for the little guy. "I must have been." She glanced at the small plastic shovel in his hand. "What are you doing out here?" She glanced around for a sign of an adult or someone the boy might have been playing with, but the yard was empty, the last guest having checked out that morning at the request of Victoria and Luke.

"Looking for a place to plant Mom and Dad," he said quietly.

Lindsay frowned. She had no idea what that meant. She wasn't sure how much the boys understood about death and the fact their parents were gone, and she didn't know where to start to explain it further. "I'm not sure I understand."

"You know, like Elmer."

Elmer? "Sweetie, who's Elmer?"

"He was our guinea pig. When he died, we dug a hole and buried him right over there, and now he's growing into that tree." He pointed across the yard to a maple seedling standing about a foot high.

The family had planted a tree in honor of their pet. She vaguely remembered being invited to Elmer's funeral last year, but she'd had to work.

"So, where do you think?" He stood and scanned the yard.

She pulled him to her and gave him a big hug. "Hey, do you remember Grandpa and Grandma Connelly and how they are buried in the cemetery?"

"Yeah, we visit them every Christmas and put flowers on the rock."

The headstone. She smiled sadly. "Exactly. Well, I think your mom and dad would like to be there with them."

He frowned and then glanced at his shovel. "But what about the tree? Grandpa and Grandma didn't grow into a tree."

This was so tough. "We can plant two

trees…next to Elmer…in memory of your mom and dad. Would that be okay?"

He nodded, his sad smile returning. "I'll go find a spot."

"Okay." She watched him run off toward the maple tree.

The sound of the screen door opening behind her made her sigh. She didn't have the energy to go another round with her mother right now. But as she turned, it was her father who stepped outside, his gaze on Jacob.

His speech was muffled but "You did good" was clear enough to bring tears to her eyes.

CHAPTER FOUR

AT THE BACK of the room, once the funeral service was over, Lindsay struggled with the desire to flee as she received the condolences of each of the Brookhollow family and friends in attendance. The overwhelming smell of lilies in the small space was making her sick.

"I had seen them hours before…" Doug Miller was saying to her father. His wife, Marge, was nodding and repeating the same phrase: "Such a senseless tragedy."

On her right, her mother spoke to Father Paul, whose sermon had been as uplifting as possible, given the circumstances. To Lindsay, it had sounded as though he was making excuses. "We can never understand or question His intent," he was saying now. She forced herself to tune out the sound of his voice.

He was right about that. She could never—

would never—understand how this had happened.

After the Millers passed them, she turned to her mother. "I'll be back in a few minutes. I'm going to go check on the kids." Rachel's cousin Leigh and her husband, Logan, were sitting with them until everyone returned to the bed-and-breakfast where Victoria and her mother had arranged for refreshments.

She found the kids with the couple in the hallway outside the sanctuary. "Hi, guys," she said, her voice hoarse. Crying herself to sleep every night after the kids finally settled in their parent's bed had left her exhausted and weak.

"They didn't want to stay inside any longer," Leigh said, smoothing Melissa's hair. The girl was curled up next to her on the bench, her eyes closed, but clearly awake. The boys sat across from them with Logan, and the twins were asleep in their double stroller next to him.

"That's okay, I didn't, either. You two can go now, thank you."

Leigh frowned. "You sure? We can help get them back to the B and B."

"No, I've got it. The rain hasn't started yet, so I think I'll walk back with them."

"What about the gravesite?" Logan asked.

"No!" Melissa yelled, bolting upright on the seat, panicked.

Lindsay knelt in front of her. "Shh. Don't worry, sweetheart, we're not going." She hugged her. "I think it might be too hard," she told Leigh over her niece's head. *On the kids and also on her.*

She didn't often attend funerals. In fact, she'd skipped both of her grandmothers' several years earlier. To her, once people were gone, it was too late. At least with her grandmothers, there had been time and an opportunity to say goodbye.

"Aunt Lindsay, I feel sick," Caleb said, a hand on his stomach.

So did she. She took his hand. "Would you like to go with Leigh and Logan in their car?"

He nodded.

"How about you, Jacob?"

"I want to stay with Caleb," the boy said sadly.

Luke had been right. The kids had banded

together over the past few days, rarely leaving their rooms. Even the babies seemed to know something was confusing and had been quieter, sleeping more during the day and waking restlessly at night.

"The boys can come with us and we'll meet you there?" Leigh said, standing.

"Thanks Leigh...Logan."

Stepping outside a moment later, she pushed the double stroller across the full parking lot as Melissa fell into step beside her. The child who had barely spoken in three days now said, "When were you going to tell us we're going to go live with Grandma and Grandpa?" The anger and hurt in the young voice was unmistakable.

Lindsay stopped abruptly and stooped to Melissa's eye level. "Nothing is decided yet."

She hadn't mentioned her parents' idea to the children because she had no idea what to do. Her parents were right: she didn't know anything about raising children...and five had been a challenge for two parents, let alone one. But the thought of moving them to Phoenix made her nauseous.

Rachel and Nathan had named her and Ben legal guardians, and so far no one had even heard from Ben. She brushed the anger she felt about that aside.

"I don't want to leave our home."

"I know, sweetheart. And I'd love to tell you things won't change, but I'm not sure what's going to happen."

Even if the kids stayed in Brookhollow with her, they would have to leave the B and B. She had a house—which wasn't quite big enough—and a career. How would she be able to do this?

Melissa's shoulders started to shake. Lindsay bent even lower to hug her. "I'm sorry. We will figure this out, okay?" She smoothed the girl's hair, praying for the answers she didn't have.

"How could they leave us, Aunt Lindsay?" she whispered.

How many times had she asked herself that question in the past few days?

"It wasn't their choice, sweetheart. They loved you very much and they would never have left you if they'd had a choice."

Melissa pulled away and wiped her eyes. "You have a choice."

HOW MUCH LONGER were these people going to stay?

With uncertain steps, Lindsay moved through the crowded room. She understood this tradition of gathering when the person who'd passed had been old...or sick for a long time, but when the passing was sudden and there were five children to consider, wouldn't the best way to pay respects be to give the family privacy?

By now her mother had made sure everyone knew that Lindsay had been appointed legal guardian of the kids, and the responses ranged from murmured discussions and questioning looks to the outright bluntness of her aunt Muriel. "Were they out of their minds?"

The consensus was the same: she was the last person anyone would have expected Nathan to name as guardian in his will. Apparently the only thing that sensible, practical Nathan had ever done that perplexed people was to leave the well-being of his children to his flighty, inconsistent sister.

The never-ending supply of hors d'oeuvres, desserts and finger sandwiches kept coming from the kitchen, but she had no appetite. She wished the food would run out so maybe these people would all finally go home.

She'd barely seen the kids in hours as her mother took them around to various friends and family members who had arrived from out of town. "They want to offer their condolences," she'd said when Lindsay suggested giving the children a break.

The kids looked tired, confused and lost. All of the emotions she felt were mirrored on their tiny faces.

Melissa caught her eye and her desperation was too much for Lindsay. Crossing the room, she took her niece by the hand.

"Where are you going?" her mother asked.

"Aunt Muriel was looking for her," she lied, giving the girl's hand a squeeze.

"Oh, okay. Well, make sure she meets Uncle…"

Yeah, she'd get right on that, Lindsay

thought as she led Melissa away and up the stairs.

"Thanks," Melissa said once they were inside her bedroom.

"Sorry, I didn't do it sooner." She hugged her. "How are you doing?"

"I'd like to be alone if that's okay," Melissa said, sitting on the pink-and-white quilt Rachel's grandma Norris had made for her in honor of being the first great-grandchild. On the bed was her self-made family photo album, a purple scrapbook decorated with flowers and hearts.

"Of course, sweetheart. If you need me, text me, okay?" She'd bought a prepaid cell phone for her niece against her parents' wishes the month before. At the time they'd lectured her about it, but today she was grateful for the phone. "I'll make sure no one bothers you," she said just as there was a knock on the door.

No freaking way, Mom.

She swung open the door, ready to blast her mother if she insisted Melissa rejoin the guests downstairs, but it was Jacob and Caleb standing there. "Hi, guys." She quickly scanned the hall as they entered, making sure her mother wasn't close behind.

"We ran away from Grandma," Caleb said.

"Can we stay in here with Mel?" Jacob asked.

Lindsay glanced at Melissa. "That's up to your sister."

"It's fine," she said, tucking the photo album under her pillow.

"Okay. Are you guys hungry? I can sneak up some food."

All three shook their heads.

"Yeah, me, neither," she said, moving out into the hall. At this rate they'd all weigh a collective hundred pounds by week's end. "Text if you need anything." Closing the door, she leaned against it and shut her eyes.

At the sound of footfalls coming up the stairs, she ducked into the bathroom across the hall, locked the door quickly and slid the length of it to the floor.

If the kids could hide from her mother for a while, so could she.

"I'LL JUST BE A SEC," Lindsay called through the door of the bathroom.

Noah leaned against the wall and waited. He'd seen her go in there almost ten minutes ago and he'd resisted the urge to check on her for—he looked at his watch—nine minutes and thirty-eight seconds.

The past few days had been torture as he'd tried to be there for her but not intrude on the family's time. The drive from the Newark airport to Brookhollow with her parents had made it painfully obvious she was not close to them. In fact, her mother seemed to blame her for not being able to save Nathan.

He'd never met the Harpers before that day, and if he never had to spend time with them again, it would be too soon. Seeing the way they treated their only daughter had made him angry for her.

She, on the other hand, had accepted the verbal abuse from her mother. And whether it was because she wanted to avoid an argument in front of him or if she actually believed there was truth in her mother's harsh criticism, he wasn't sure.

Either way, seeing the outspoken woman

he cared about so quiet and defeated had torn him up.

He heard the water run and then a few muffled sniffles before the door opened. "Hi," he said as she stepped out, her eyes bloodshot, sunken and dark.

"Hey, Noah. It's all yours," she said, moving past him.

"Lindsay…" In a second his arms were around her, hugging her tight to his chest.

She sank against him for a moment before straightening and taking a step back. "I should get back down there. I've been gone long enough."

He pulled her back into him. "Take all the time you need. There's no rush."

Mrs. Mason, Victoria's mother, was making sure everyone had everything they needed. He'd noticed her insisting Lindsay eat and rest a few times so far that day and he loved her already. He just wished Lindsay's own mother was as sensitive.

"I need to check on the kids."

"All asleep." He knew that because, while Lindsay had been hiding in the washroom, he'd seen Leigh put the babies down for a nap.

He'd also pretended to check Melissa's room for Lindsay's mother when she'd been combing the hallway for them just moments before. Of course he'd lied and told her they weren't in there. They had all fallen asleep on Melissa's bed.

"You should get some sleep, too. You look exhausted." He tilted her face up to stare into her eyes. "And when was the last time you ate something?"

She shook her head. "I remember that sandwich you brought me at the clinic the other night...and the potato salad."

"Let's get you something." He rubbed her arms, but she just shook her head.

"I'm not hungry," she said, moving away from him. Her gaze fell to the floor. "Thank you, Noah, for checking on me."

He took her shaky hands in his steady ones. "Look at me," he said quietly, and waited for her gaze to meet his. "You're not alone. I'm here... Whenever, wherever... Just say the word, Lindsay, and I'm here."

He knew despite his relentless pursuit of her over the past year, that she still didn't take his affection seriously. He needed her to see him as someone she could rely on. It didn't even terrify him that he wanted to be that person for her. Since the day he'd met Lindsay, he'd been head over heels for her.

"Why would you do that?" she croaked.

He touched her cheek, letting the back of his hand trail along her jawline as he cupped her face between his hands. "I thought that would be obvious by now, but if it isn't..." He lowered his lips until they softly grazed hers.

As her eyes closed slowly, she gripped his shoulders and he felt her body relax into him. He tightened his arms around her, pulling her closer.

"At your brother's funeral? Seriously, Lindsay?" Pamela Harper said from behind them in the hall.

Lindsay's eyes flew open and she jumped back, the back of her hand going to her mouth.

"Mom!"

Standing between the two women, his arm protectively around Lindsay, Noah started to say, "I was just—"

"Taking advantage perhaps?" Pamela glared at them. "Though, knowing my daughter, probably not." She shook her head.

A shiver ran through him and his first instinct was to defend Lindsay, but her hand on his forearm kept him from speaking.

"I was just coming back downstairs, Mom."

Her mother held out a hand to stop her. "Wait. I need to talk to you." She turned to Noah. "Can you give us a minute, please?"

He squeezed Lindsay's hand and kissed her cheek. "I meant what I said—anything you need." He nodded stiffly at Pamela as he passed her and turned the corner of the hallway, pausing when he heard her say, "About the kids."

What about the kids?

"Not now, Mom." Lindsay's voice was strained. "This is not the time."

"But it's the time to be kissing some strange man?"

"He's not a strange man. He picked you up at the airport three days ago, remember? Besides, he was checking to make sure I was okay."

The edge in her voice made him realize he'd probably been the only one over the past few days, besides Mrs. Mason, who'd showed concern for Lindsay. He wished he'd been able to do more.

"We need to make a decision and I think you know what the right thing to do is."

"Mom, can we please talk about this later? Once the guests are gone? Tomorrow?"

"Your father and I are flying out tomorrow morning."

There was a moment of silence before Lindsay said, "You're…leaving already?"

"Yes. Your father isn't doing so well, and the stress of all of this isn't helping. There's no reason for us to stay any longer."

For Lindsay. Noah fought the urge to join the conversation and remind this woman she hadn't lost both of her children in the crash.

"You're right. There's no reason to stay," Lindsay said coldly, but there was something else in her voice. Strength. "I've made a decision, so there's nothing to talk about. The kids are staying with me."

"I THOUGHT YOU QUIT." Noah's voice behind her made her jump as she hid the cigarette in her trembling hand later that evening.

"And I'll quit again tomorrow," she said,

watching him walk across the yard to the gazebo in the backyard of the B and B. So much for not being discovered out here among the shaded privacy of the trees.

Reluctantly she snuffed out the first cigarette she'd had in weeks as he took a seat next to her.

"I thought everyone had left."

After she'd put the kids to bed in their parents' room, where they still insisted on sleeping, there had only been a few remaining guests in the sitting room with her mother and she hadn't wanted to join them. Not for any money.

Her mother's friends were sure to pressure her to let the kids move to Phoenix with her parents. Melissa wanted to stay in Brookhollow and so did the boys. They had friends here, family here.

Their parents were here.

"Only a few women left inside. I was about to leave when I saw you sneak out here and thought maybe you could use some company."

What she wanted was to be alone. Alone to try to figure out how she was going to take care of five children. The last thing she needed right now was to have to explain to Noah the kiss they'd shared earlier that day —that she'd been hurting and he'd offered comfort, that was all.

She remained silent, staring out over the yard as the early June sun set in the sky.

"I overheard your conversation with your mom," he said quietly.

She'd suspected as much. "I really don't have the energy to talk about it right now."

He nodded. "Okay." He ran his hands along the length of his dark dress pants and hesitated before saying, "If it makes you feel any better, I think you're doing the right thing."

Unexpectedly annoyed, she snapped at him. "Really? You think the kids staying with their clueless aunt is the right thing? Obviously you know nothing about me."

"I know you're kind, caring, loving…and a great aunt to those kids," he said.

"Exactly—a great aunt. That's what I am. The cool aunt who pisses off their parents by letting them eat too much sugar and letting Melissa stay up well past bedtime. Not exactly mother material."

"That was because you were their aunt, so no one expected you to discipline them or to be anything else. But now—"

She held up a hand to cut him off. She couldn't hear this. She knew all too well that her role with the kids would have to change. She just had no idea how to make the transition. "Seriously, Noah, I can't."

He clamped his mouth shut. They sat in silence for a long moment before he reached for her hand.

Pulling it back, she stood. "I think I'll call it a night." He obviously had no plans to leave her to her thoughts and a repeat of earlier was not happening if that's what he expected.

"Did I say something wrong? Because that wasn't my intent." He also stood, shoving his hands into his pockets.

She sighed. "No. Look, thank you for everything you've done, but I really don't think you're the person I should be leaning on right now."

"Why not me? I want to be here." He touched her arm and she backed away.

"Noah, I'm sorry I kissed you. That was wrong. I told you I wasn't going to date you before and I'm certainly not changing my mind now."

"Because of the kids."

"Yes...no... *Yes!* Come on—I'm a woman with five children now. Look at me. This is who I am." She pointed to her shoulder where Abby had vomited an hour before. "Feel my hair."

He did.

"Chocolate cookie. I have to learn to be this new person now, for the kids. I have no idea how I'm going to do it. But I'm going to because that's all I care about."

He started to speak but she cut him off again.

"I have no room for a guy like you in my life. A guy who gets hurt and hurts people for money."

She stepped out of the gazebo, not wanting to see his stricken expression. Knowing she'd hit him below the belt. "Good night, Noah. Thank you for being here."

"Lindsay, I'm not giving up. If you need me, I'm still here," he called after her.

She didn't stop walking.

"You're an MMA fighter, Noah. You know even less than I do about raising children, and I need to think long-term daddy potential if and whenever I decide to date again."

She refused to look back to see the effect of the damage she was inflicting.

"Once again, you're not the right guy."

CHAPTER FIVE

LINDSAY SAT IN her Jeep staring at the sign for Brent's Dodge, her depression at an all-time low. *I can't do this.* She'd ordered the Jeep from the Chrysler dealership in New York two years before. Leather seats, six-CD player, hardtop with a sunroof and painted a deep purple, it had been customized for her.

But three seats, five kids… She wasn't great at math, but even she knew that wasn't going to work.

She sighed as she opened the door and climbed out, sliding her dark sunglasses over her eyes.

"Hi. Welcome to Brent's Dodge," said a man in a dark charcoal suit, extending a hand to her. His nametag read Brent Cooper, Owner and Sales Manager.

"Hi," she said, scanning the lot. The selection wasn't as great as she'd been hoping.

"What can we help you with?" he asked with a smile.

If she had to guess, he was probably her age or slightly older and, based on the tailored suit and expensive watch he wore, business at the dealership was good.

"Minivans," she mumbled, wishing the ground would open up and swallow her. The one vehicle she swore she'd never own.

"Okay. Over here we have the Dodge Grand Caravans that arrived last week," Brent said, leading her toward the new vehicles.

Lindsay stopped him. "I'm thinking of a used vehicle, if you have anything in stock."

"Used minivans?"

She cringed. *Go ahead, Nathan, you can say "I told you so" now.* She nodded.

"Well, we don't see many. When folks buy a van, they rarely trade them in on a regular basis. Not much point really. I mean, with kids making a mess in the back seat or dogs tearing up the upholstery..."

He stopped when he registered the look on her face.

"But we do have a few over here," he

added, taking her to the far end of the lot where a Previously Enjoyed Inventory trailer was set up. "I'm the new-car sales manager, so let me grab Doug for you." Brent climbed the stairs to the trailer and opened the door.

While she waited, Lindsay scanned her options. A dark blue Chevrolet Uplander or a red Nissan Quest. Both looked well used. Never in a million years would she have expected to be standing in the used-vehicle section of a dealership trying to decide between ugly and uglier.

She peered through the window of the Nissan. The driver's side leather seat was slightly torn and the carpet in the back looked stained and worn—the dog Brent must have been referring to.

Please let the other one be better.

She held her breath as she studied the blue Chevrolet. It looked almost brand-new on the inside with upholstery on the seats instead of leather and a dark charcoal interior she hoped would hide damage and dirt better. She breathed a sigh of relief, despite the single CD player and the standard windows.

"Hi, I'm Doug Cooper, the used-car manager," said a tall, thin man. Despite the June heat, he was wearing a Windbreaker-style dealership jacket over his polo shirt and dress pants. His comb-over flapped slightly in the breeze and the faint smell of cigarettes followed him like a haze.

She breathed it in deeply, realized what she was doing and shook her head.

Doug Cooper had to be a relative of Brent's, obviously, though she couldn't find any resemblance between the two men. "I thought they were called 'previously enjoyed'?"

He laughed, revealing a few missing teeth. "Right. And last year, they were called 'pre-owned,' the year before that 'lightly travelled.' All means the same and until they decide on one term and stick to it, my business card says Used-Car Manager."

He handed her one of his cards.

"See anything you like?"

She glanced toward the new Charger across the lot. "Yes…but, unfortunately, I need a minivan." She almost choked on the word.

"Sorry to say, we have little to choose

from right now. They are what we like to call lifer vehicles. You know, you buy one and have it for life…or until the kids move out," he said with a laugh.

She cringed. Here we go again.

"You starting a family?" he asked, glancing at her stomach.

More like trying to survive being handed one. "Sort of. Anyway, the blue one? How much?" She hoped it was in her price range. Paying even more than she planned for something she didn't want would be torture.

"Sticker price is fifteen thousand."

Five more than she'd been hoping to pay. She knew the blue-book price for her Jeep would be about ten or eleven and she still owed several grand on the financing. "Any wiggle room?"

He winked and it was more of a double-eye blink. "Always. You got a trade?"

"Yes. A 2011 Jeep Wrangler."

He studied her. "Can't fit a car seat or two in the back?"

"Can't fit two car seats, two booster seats and a moody preteen in the back."

His eyes widened then his expression

took on a blend of sympathy and admiration. "Wow…okay…let's make this work for you."

He reached into his pocket for his cigarettes. "I've been dying for one of these. You smoke?" he asked, extending the pack toward her.

"I do today."

"I STILL CAN'T believe Ben didn't even make it to the funeral," Lily said a week later, sitting in the dining room at the bed-and-breakfast, which Victoria had closed to guests until they had time to adjust and figure out what to do next.

The kids had finally settled down for the night and Lindsay could barely keep her eyes open. Double shifts at the clinic had never left her feeling as drained as taking care of five children every day. Thankfully she had Leigh, who'd helped her with the boys that week, letting them play with the other children at her day care next door.

Dealing with Melissa's adjustment to her parents' death and the twin girls, who were teething and being potty-trained was challenging enough. Three disgusting accidents that week and she'd caved and bought the training pull-ups Rachel had been trying to avoid using.

Sorry, Rach. You were a brilliant mother and I'm just a crappy substitute.

"I mean not only was he Nathan's friend and business partner, but he's the other legal guardian as godfather." Lily shook her head.

"He's only really been godfather in name only, as far as I can tell. He rarely visits. They usually go to him in Newark, in his big, fancy house. The kids always come back with tons of gifts..." Lindsay shrugged. "I don't know. Maybe Nathan didn't really expect him to step up." She sipped her wine. Her nightly glass had turned into her reward for making it through the day.

"Has he even called? Once?"

"No." But she was almost relieved. She already had too many decisions to make regarding the kids and their future. Trying to incorporate someone else into her plans would be difficult. "I remember Rachel saying something a few weeks ago about him and Nathan being at odds about a new client or something." She shrugged. "Whatever. It's not like I need him."

What she needed was an army to help her put things back on track for her and the kids, but for now she'd settle for coming to at least one firm decision. Every time she thought she'd made one, doubt—aka her mother's voice—shook her confidence.

"Has Melissa gone back to school yet?" Lily tucked her legs under her on the couch.

"No. It's been less than two weeks. I'm giving her more time. In fact, school's out soon, I may not send her back at all until September."

Lily clamped her mouth shut.

"You don't think that's a good idea?"

"Who knows what a good idea is at this point, Linds? I just think maybe it might help her to be around her friends and not hiding in her bedroom all day. Get her mind off her parents for a little while."

"Maybe…I don't know. I'll add it to the list of things I'm probably going to screw up in these children's lives." Her chest tightened and she forced another sip of wine.

Lily offered a sympathetic smile. "You're going to do fine."

"I killed that cactus you gave me for my birthday."

Lily shook her head and smiled. "A cactus is a dumb plant anyway. Do they need water? Don't they need water?" Suddenly she looked serious again. "When are you going to tell them about moving?"

Good question. The one firm decision she had made was that she needed to move the kids to her house sooner rather than later. The three oldest were still sleeping in their parents' bed every night and she always fell asleep in the chair beside them. Not good for them and not good for her.

She only had another week off work and her job was too critical for her to be falling asleep on her feet.

She shivered. The thought of returning to the clinic after the accident made her uneasy. "I'll tell them tomorrow...or this weekend." She bit her lip.

Lily shot her a look.

"Okay, tomorrow. They are going to hate

me." She buried her face in the crook of her arm resting on the table in front of her.

"No, they won't. They might be upset about leaving their home, but without Rachel and Nathan, this isn't their home anymore anyway. The six of you have to build a new home."

Six of you.

From one to six. Just like that.

NOAH LAY STARING at his ceiling, his heavy duvet pulled high up around his neck, despite it being summer. A chill ran through him and the back of his head throbbed. If he didn't know any better, he'd swear he'd been run over by a truck.

Reluctantly removing one arm from under the covers, he reached for his watch on the bedside table, squinting in the early morning sunlight. Eight-thirty. He had half an hour before he was supposed to meet Dominic at the community center.

Joanne had also mentioned that she was bringing along another volunteer from the MENTOR program who was interested in getting involved—a certified social worker.

He wanted to be there to show this new person around and hopefully convince them to donate some of their time. The program needed it. Maybe with more staff, he'd be able to spend a little less time there and focus more on training in the coming weeks.

Time to man up.

He tossed the duvet back and immediately goose bumps covered his body. Rubbing his arms for warmth, he noticed that while he may be freezing his flesh was hot to the touch. He felt his forehead. Scorching. Great, a fever. A month away from his next fight, he didn't have time to be sick. He pushed himself up from the bed and ignored the muscle-aching pain shooting through his legs and back. A hot shower was all he needed. Turning the water as high as he could, he removed his boxer briefs and climbed in. Ten minutes later, knowing he would soon drain the boiler of any heat, he reluctantly turned off the taps and climbed out. Even the plush towel felt rough against his skin as he tied it at his waist and made his way to the kitchenette in the bachelor-suite apartment. Opening his fridge, he removed a bottle of Gatorade and took a gulp, then winced as razor blades coursed down his throat. He reached for his neck and felt the swollen glands. Fantastic, he really was sick.

Maybe he should call Joanne and let her know he wouldn't make it in. He didn't want to pass this on to any of the kids at the community center.

No. He had to go. New volunteers were rare, especially qualified ones from the MENTOR program; he couldn't miss this meeting. Pulling on his jeans and a T-shirt, Noah grabbed his wallet and keys and headed for the door. With the program already on thin ice and lacking stability with his absence, he needed to be there when he said he would be. He hoped this new volunteer saw the value of the Turnaround program as much as he did.

"HEY, CARL, HAVE you seen Dominic?" Noah asked as he entered the hall a few moments later. He'd checked the outside basketball and tennis courts, but the teenager had been nowhere around. He didn't appear to be inside, either.

"No, haven't seen him at all today." The tutor from the high school shrugged as he set up a table with calculators and sample math tests for the kids writing their assessment exams for summer school the following morning.

Dominic never missed a week. Noah hoped he hadn't already given the kid whatever flu virus was destroying his body. He coughed and it felt as if his throat was on fire. "So, how is everything going?" he asked Carl, his voice scratchy.

"Okay. The ones that really want help are doing great. The ones who don't…" He shrugged.

"We do what we can," he said, even though he wanted to punch somebody.

Joanne smiled at him through the office window, and noticing another woman with her, he relaxed a little. Getting interested volunteers to show up was half the battle.

An hour later, feeling confident that they'd just recruited the social worker for the program, he shut off the bike in the driveway of Dominic's four-plex housing unit near the highway. A couple of teenagers sat on the shared front deck, smoking, as one of them fixed a rusted chain on a ten-speed bike on the lawn.

Smoking. That habit hadn't been "cool" since the seventies. It amazed him kids still even *started* the disgusting habit.

He thought of Lindsay, smoking the night of the funeral, and wondered how long she'd been a smoker. And how he could help her kick it without driving her crazy.

"Hey, guys," he said, walking up the gravel path toward the house.

The oldest boy nodded, folding his thin arms as menacingly as possible across his chest. "You a cop?"

"No, a friend of Dominic's. He around?"

"Upstairs, I think," the boy said, eyeing the motorcycle.

Reaching into his pocket, Noah retrieved a twenty-dollar bill and handed it over. "Make sure she's sitting there when I come out."

The boy's eyes lit up as he tucked the

money into his cigarette pack. "You got it, man."

Noah opened the front door and took the wooden staircase two steps at a time. The smell of pot in the hallway was overwhelming and a stack of beer-bottle boxes stood against the wall. He knew this scene all too well. He'd gotten out…away from something similar…barely. He'd hoped he could help Dominic do the same. He knocked on the door. "Hello, Ms. Cage?"

The door opened a second later and Marilyn Cage smiled when she saw him. "Noah." She let him in then gave him a big hug. "Great to see you."

"You, too. How have you been?" The home was spotless and, unlike the smell in the hallway, inside the tempting aroma of homemade chicken soup made his mouth water. He hadn't eaten since the night before.

"Good…tired a lot as usual."

Dominic's mother had lupus and it drained her strength. Though it didn't seem to stop her from keeping her home clean and cooking for her and Dominic. He admired the woman for doing her best with the situation she found herself in.

Dominic's father had a gambling addiction and had left the family when the boy was seven. Alone and dealing with an illness that prevented her from working many hours, Marilyn and Dominic had been forced to give up their home in a better part of town.

"Is Dominic home? I was expecting him at the community center today." He covered a cough with his arm.

She frowned. "You sound awful. Let me give you some soup and I'll get Dom. He's in his bedroom."

He knew it was no use to argue on the soup, and he was dying for it anyway. "Thanks, Ms. Cage."

Going into the kitchen, he sat at the small table and, noticing the unsteady way it shifted to the right, he bent to look at the table legs. Unscrewing one, he readjusted the height and secured it in place. He nudged the table: solid. Good, he'd at least earned his soup.

"Hey, Noah," Dominic said, appearing in

faded Superman pajama pants and a light blue shirt.

Noah glanced at his watch. "It's almost ten. Pajamas? You sick?"

"Nah, just hanging around." The boy shrugged.

"Well, you're supposed to be hanging around at the center. I dragged my sick butt out of bed to meet you," he said.

Marilyn set two bowls of soup on the table in front of them, and offered Noah a bread roll.

"Thank you," Noah said, dipping it into the soup.

Dominic sat across from him, but didn't touch his soup. "Sorry, didn't feel like it."

"Okay, so tell me, how did the test go?" He held his breath as he waited.

"I passed."

"That's great!"

The kid shrugged again.

"I don't get it. Why aren't you more excited?" Dominic had tried three times to pass the test. He should be jumping over the moon now.

"It's not like it matters or anything." He slumped lower in the chair.

"Why not?"

"I can't afford a car."

Marilyn's face fell.

"Not right now, but eventually. Besides, I told you I'd teach you to drive the motorcycle." His head felt like a hundred pounds on his shoulders and his eyes were barely staying open, but a promise was a promise.

"You mean the motorcycle that was just boosted from the driveway?"

The sound of his bike roaring down the street made him jump up, spilling the hot soup on the tablecloth. "Sorry, Marilyn. I'll clean that—"

"Don't worry about it, go get your bike," she said, already cleaning up the mess.

Swinging open the door, Noah rode the banister to the bottom of the stairs and burst through the front door. Turning to the kid he'd paid to watch his bike, he said, "Hey, man, my bike?"

"Linc's only taking it for a spin, he'll bring it back." The kid shrugged.

"I paid you to keep an eye on it." He

couldn't believe this. Hands on his hips, he scanned the street, but there was no sign of his motorcycle or this Linc.

"You said make sure it was here when you came out. You didn't say not to drive it in the meantime, and we didn't think you'd be out so quick."

"Ah, there's the man I was waiting for. Maybe now we can get some of these heavier items moved," Luke said, slapping Jim on the back just as Noah's motorcycle pulled into the B and B that evening.

"Hey! I'd like to help, but you know I hurt my back bowling the other night," Jim said.

"Sorry, I forgot you were an old man," Luke replied.

Lindsay smiled at the friends' exchange. She set a box of clothing inside the minivan and felt her cheeks flush as she watched Noah remove his helmet and turn off the bike.

"You asked Noah to help?"

Despite his offer to help with anything she may need him for, she hadn't spoken to him since the funeral. Since the kiss and harsh words in the gazebo.

She didn't want to rely on Noah...or anyone...but especially not Noah. What good could come of that?

The idea of dating anyone at all was almost comical...in a dark comedy sort of way.

"Yeah. Is that okay? I saw him this morning when I was on my way to pick up the moving van and he offered his burly biceps and superhuman strength." Luke grinned, watching as her cheeks flushed an even deeper shade of pink, she was sure.

"Oh...okay. Yeah...it's fine." She tried to look busy as Noah approached.

"Hey, sorry I'm late. I had to wait for my motorcycle to be returned to me," he said.

She frowned. "Huh?"

"Never mind." He touched her cheek. "How are you?"

Stressed, exhausted and not at all sure she was doing the right thing. "I'm good."

He studied her and she didn't believe for a second he'd bought her lie, but he squeezed her shoulder gently and said, "Great to hear that." His eyes held hers a second too long and she glanced away. "I'm here and ready to work. Where can I start?"

"I need help moving the crib pieces out of the girls' room," Luke told him, climbing the front stairs.

"Sure," Noah returned. But once Luke disappeared inside, he hesitated and looked at Lindsay. "How are you really doing?"

May as well be honest. "I'm surviving."

"It will get better."

"I don't think so, but I like your optimism," she said.

He took her hands in his and bent lower to look at her. "Remember—what doesn't kill us…"

"Makes us stronger?"

He shook his head. "No. Hurts like hell, until one day it hurts a little less."

Her pulse soared as his grip tightened around her hands and he placed a kiss on her forehead. How easy it would be to give in to this strong, handsome, kind man in front of her, whom she believed was sincere in his offer to help. But to what end?

What kind of father figure would an

MMA fighter make? She pulled her hands away and forced a wry laugh. "Well, right now, I need to figure out a way to get Melissa to come out of her bedroom. She locked herself in last night. Stupid interior locks on these B and B doors," she mumbled in frustration.

No amount of coaxing had worked. At one point she'd even resolved to the number-one what-not-to-do parenting rule and tried bribery. She'd been desperate. "Actually, I can probably help with that," he said. "Got a screwdriver?"

Twenty minutes later, the door off the hinges, Lindsay came face-to-face with an angry eight-year-old. Her momentary relief at the door being opened shattered instantly at the sight of her niece's glare. "You can't make me leave. This is my home."

Lindsay swallowed hard. This wasn't going to be easy. Nathan had been right when he'd said Mel was more like her than she was her own mother. The stubborn independence she admired in the child was now probably going to be her greatest challenge.

One she wasn't sure she was ready for. "I think this will be the best thing…"

"What do you know, Aunt Lindsay? Do you even know how to take care of us? If we wanted to leave, we could have gone with Grandma and Grandpa." Melissa folded her arms across her chest and the glare remained.

The words stung after the verbal battles she'd endured with her mother to make sure that hadn't happened. "I thought you wanted to stay in Brookhollow?"

"But I want to stay here."

Well, she wanted all of this to be some big nightmare, but rarely did reality meet her expectations.

The girl had been through so much and Lindsay had known things would get harder before they had any chance of getting better.

She knelt in front of Melissa. "I know this is hard—"

"You don't know anything. Your parents are still alive!" Melissa yelled, pushing her.

Lindsay lost her balance at the same time Noah entered the room. His hands on her shoulders caught her from falling onto the hardwood floor. "Melissa, your aunt is—"

Lindsay shook her head as she stood. "I got this," she said to Noah. "I know you don't understand this right now, Melissa, but I'm trying to do the best thing for all of us. So, grab your suitcase and please start packing up your things."

Instead, the girl ran past her out into the hall. "I hate you," she yelled as she flew down the stairs.

Lindsay's chest ached, but at the same time it felt as though a weight of doubt had been lifted from her shoulders.

If they're not mad at you, you're probably not doing the job right.

"I hope you're right, Rach," she whispered.

LATER THAT EVENING, feeling worse than if he'd gone three rounds in the cage with someone twice his size, Noah pulled his motorcycle into the lot of the medical clinic. His fever had yet to break, and his vision had started to blur. He'd never been nervous on the bike before but the short drive from the B and B to the clinic had been scary.

When he'd run into Luke after leaving Dominic's that morning, there had been no way he could have said no to helping them move the children's things to Lindsay's house.

After their heated discussion in the gazebo the evening of the funeral, he'd wanted to give her some space and time to figure things out. While he battled with the desire to help her, he'd respected her wishes to not be a shoulder to cry on. But he still intended to show up in a heartbeat when needed. Even if she hadn't been the one to ask.

He opened the door to the clinic, relieved to see only one other patient waiting. Good, this wouldn't take long. Going to the desk, he announced his arrival to Rebecca, one of the nurses.

She glanced up at him over her thick, dark-rimmed green glasses. "Hi, Noah. You look awful."

Did they see any other kind around here?

"Thanks. I feel even worse." He scanned

the hallway behind the desk and noticed all of the exam room doors closed. Maybe they were busier than he thought. "How long's the wait?"

"Just a few minutes," Rebecca said, grabbing his chart from the file cabinet behind her.

Sitting in the waiting room chair, an incredible itch made his right hand lunge toward his back. Another violent attack on his arm a second later had him removing his jacket. Freeing his arm, he noticed several red dots along the inside of his bicep. A rash from sweating while moving?

His back twitched again near his shoulder and, moving his T-shirt aside, he noticed several spots there, as well. Lifting the edge of his shirt confirmed his stomach was also covered.

He approached the desk quickly, his shirt still raised.

Rebecca's eyes widened.

"What are these?" he asked in a panic.

"The most incredible set of abs I've ever seen," she said.

"These." He pointed to the row of spots

along his stomach muscles and then turned to show her the ones on his shoulder.

She smiled sympathetically. "I take it you've never had chicken pox before."

CHAPTER SIX

LINDSAY KNOCKED ON Noah's apartment door early the next morning before she could change her mind.

Chicken pox. Poor guy. It could be really awful in adults. He must have pushed through it to help her. She just hoped his good deed hadn't spread the illness to others. She would disinfect everything he'd touched as soon as she got home.

"Hang on," he called through the door, and she watched as the doorknob on her side wiggled violently, but didn't turn.

She frowned. "Is your door broken?"

"Lindsay?" The surprise in his voice almost made her regret coming.

"Yeah, I heard you were sick…"

"Can you turn the knob on your side?" he asked.

"Okay…" She turned the knob and the door opened.

On the other side, Noah stood wearing only his jeans and...

"What's with the boxing gloves?" she asked in an attempt to avert her gaze and her thoughts from his magnificent bare torso. "You're training? I thought you were sick."

He should be resting...and he should have more clothes on. A lot more clothes.

"I am. The gloves are the only way I can stop myself from scratching these annoying things," he said, gesturing to the blisters.

She laughed. Clever.

"Have you tried calamine lotion for the itch?"

"No."

"Do you have any?"

"Probably not..."

"It's okay, I brought some with me," she said, setting her purse on the counter, noticing how clean his apartment was. It was definitely cleaner than her house. She wasn't sure why it surprised her, but she'd expected...

She didn't know what to expect anymore. She handed the pink lotion to him. "It should help."

He took the bottle in his gloved hand. "Thank you."

"Sure."

He struggled to get his gloves off, then gave up and tried to work the cap with the gloves still on, then shrugged. "I'll put it on later."

She sighed as she reached for the bottle and opened it. She was a nurse, after all. "Where are they?"

"Everywhere," he mumbled.

"I'll do the ones I can see," she said, turning him around.

The sight of his muscular back and arms wasn't really a reprieve from the front view. He was all muscle—six feet of beautifully packaged muscle.

"I thought most fighters had tattoos," she said, pouring the lotion onto her finger and dabbing at the spots. His skin felt hot to the touch and she wondered if he'd taken any of the antibiotics sitting on his counter yet.

"I'm not opposed to them. I just haven't found something I wanted to permanently scar my body with."

"I wouldn't scar this body," she said, dabbing the backs of his arms.

He chuckled. "Thank you. That was a compliment, right?" He turned to face her.

"Don't get a big head over it. You have a mirror—you know you're attractive."

Attractive was an understatement.

"It's better coming from you," he said, brushing her hair away from her face as she dabbed at his chest, and stroking her cheek with the cool leather of the glove.

"There you are. That's as far as I go…" She stumbled as she took a step backward. Air, space, water: she needed all of that—right now. She set the bottle down on his counter. "Use that twice a day—it will help. And take the antibiotics."

He shook his head. "I'm not sure about those. I have to let coach see them first. I'm fighting in a few weeks and they do drug testing."

Right. His upcoming fight. He was still putting his life at risk.

"So you're just going to suffer through the chicken pox?"

"Until I can be sure they won't affect my ability to fight—yeah."

"Fine, tough guy. Suit yourself," she said before heading for the door.

"Hey, wait. Did you want to stick around... watch a movie? We could order some food."

"Not today."

"Not today...but not never?"

He was relentless. About dating her. And about fighting.

"Call me when you're better," she said, quickly shutting the door behind her.

Once again she was faced with the wrong guy at the wrong time.

She had to go home to the kids.

"I'M NOT LETTING you in," Brandon yelled through the glass door of Extreme Athletics two days later.

"Oh, come on, you've got to be kidding me. The spots are already out, I'm not contagious anymore."

That probably wasn't the complete truth. The nurse at the clinic said he would be contagious until the spots closed over, which hadn't happened yet. But with the fight scheduled in less than three weeks, he needed to train. A few days off, sitting on his sofa eating Doritos, had already made him feel soft around the middle.

Brandon locked the dead bolt and stood with his arms folded. "I've never had them, and I don't plan on getting them now."

"You're serious?" Noah readjusted his gym bag on his shoulder as the strap started to irritate the spots on his upper arm. The calamine lotion Lindsay had left for him was definitely working...though it had been better when she had applied it.

"Come on, Brandon. I need to train." He felt guilty about possibly spreading the disease, but this close to his fight, he couldn't afford time away from the gym.

"Bring a note from the clinic and then I'll let you in. You're not infecting my gym."

"Fine," Noah mumbled, walking away. Where was he supposed to train now? He couldn't risk going to the community center gym and spreading chicken pox to whatever kids in town hadn't already contracted them.

Securing his bag to the back of the motorcycle, he climbed on and started the bike. Well, if his coach wouldn't let him inside, he'd have to train the old-school way.

Ten minutes later he parked near the lake's edge across from the downtown core. In Brookhollow, that meant six professional buildings that stood higher than two stories.

He grabbed his gear and headed to the trail. One full lap around the lake would be two miles. A few laps, he'd at least get his cardio in for the day. He could hit the heavy bag at home.

The only thing he was really missing was the partners to grapple with, but he wasn't worried about his ground game. He'd won four of his six professional fights with a submission hold on the mat.

That was the thing Lindsay didn't realize about MMA. It really was a sport of skill and technique. Did guys get knocked out? Sure. But more often the fights were won by submission.

If only he could get her to come to one of his fights, she'd see for herself it wasn't as bad as she thought. But he knew that would never happen.

IT WAS A full week before Lindsay heard from Noah, although she'd caught sight of him everywhere. He'd been running on the trail across from the mayor's office, doing pull-ups on the playground equipment in the elementary school playground after the end of the day, playing football in the park with Ethan and the other firefighters. She couldn't escape the sight of him.

Her cell phone vibrated in her pocket as she signed off on a patient with a broken arm and turned to Rachel's grandmother, in for her regular blood pressure and heart rate check.

It was Noah. She should've known she couldn't escape the guy permanently.

She contemplated not answering. Letting it go to voice mail.

Who was she kidding? She was too old, too tired and too busy to play games.

"Um, Rebecca, I have to answer this. Can you put Mrs. Norris in an exam room, please?"

"Sure, no problem," Rebecca said, leading Ginger down the hallway.

"Oh, but, Lindsay..." the kids' great-grandmother interrupted. "I wanted to talk to you about maybe taking the kids for ice cream someday next week."

"Sure. Yes. Whenever you want, Ginger," Lindsay said a little too eagerly.

The older woman smiled and patted her arm as she passed. "I'll call you next week, dear."

Alone at the reception desk, Lindsay answered the vibrating phone on the fifth ring. "Hello?" she said, making sure her tone sounded busy and important.

"Hey, it's Noah," he said.

"Noah, hi. I have another call coming in, can I put you on hold?"

"Sure."

Lindsay hit the mute button and set the phone on the reception desk. Getting up, she went to the staff lounge and filled the coffeemaker with water. Then waited for it to brew.

She carried a cup back to the desk. She waited another minute then picked it up. "Noah, you still there?"

"Yeah." He sounded annoyed. "Important call?"

"Sorry, I've got to run…talk to you later, okay?"

Before she could hang up, he quickly asked, "Can I take you out tonight?"

"Yes."

What had she just said? What was wrong with her?

She could've banged her head with the phone.

The truth was she was desperate for an evening out. The kids and work had been her life for a month now and she needed a break, however brief.

"Yes? Really?" He laughed. "I'll pick you up at seven."

As LINDSAY REMOVED the last curler from her freshly highlighted hair, she fought to control her excitement. After work, she'd gone to Lily's shop to buy the yellow halter dress she'd picked out the week before.

"Are you sure?" Lily had asked. "I mean for months you've been turning him down, when there was just his career choice standing in the way. Now there's so much more to consider."

"I know. He's definitely Mr. Wrong. But it's just a night out, Lily. I *need* a night out."

And she had Victoria lined up to babysit—she wasn't going to lose this opportunity.

In truth, the kids were precisely the reason she'd said yes to Noah.

She had to get better at this parenting thing. Had to stop acting like the carefree, single woman she'd once been.

But for now, she needed a break.

Lindsay sighed as she stared at her reflection in the mirror. She couldn't seem to conceal the dark shadows that had first appeared under her eyes a month ago. And despite the new highlights in her hair, her recent strands of gray poked through.

At the sound of the doorbell she frowned and checked her watch. It was only ten after six.

Picking up her cell phone, she texted Go away, I'm still contemplating canceling on you.

The doorbell rang again.

Then she got a text: I'm not there yet and there's no way you're getting out of this.

Must be Victoria at the door, she thought,

putting her mascara aside. She made her way down the hall, wrapping her thin, silk bathrobe around her.

Her friend was reaching for the buzzer again as she opened the door.

Immediately, Lindsay knew something was wrong. The other woman's face was white and her eyes were wide. "Come in," she said, moving back.

"I'm in labor," Victoria said, her pitch about an octave higher than normal.

Of course she was. Impeccable timing as usual, she thought wryly.

"How far apart are the contractions?"

How much time they had was by far the most important thing to figure out. She could deliver the baby in her house if necessary, but she sure didn't want to.

"About four minutes," Victoria said, pacing frantically. "Ow, here comes another one." She bent at the waist and closed her eyes.

"Bending only makes it worse," Lindsay said, supporting the panting woman.

As a nurse, she saw it all on a daily basis, but she was the first one to opt out of the delivery room whenever possible. Births terrified her. Beautiful when they were over, absolutely devastating to watch.

"Did I hear Aunt Vic—" Melissa paused halfway into the living room. "Uh-oh, I know that look. Tell me when the gross stuff is over!" She turned and headed out.

A lot of help the eight-year-old would have been had this happened an hour from now. What had she been thinking, asking an overdue pregnant woman to babysit tonight?

As the contraction passed, she led Victoria to the couch, but reached for a blanket to cover her white leather upholstery before seating her. Like the Jeep, the furniture wasn't kid-approved and would soon have to be replaced.

"Where's Luke?"

"Newark."

Newark. Good—only two hours away. He could still potentially make it. Picking up her phone, she hesitated.

"You'll have to call him," she said handing the phone to Victoria.

Luke had changed his number years ago and hadn't given her the new one.

"And maybe block the call," she added. "He'll never answer if he sees my number."

Victoria dialed while Lindsay rushed into her bedroom to get dressed. She sighed as she saw the yellow sundress hanging on her closet door. She had thirty-eight minutes to get Victoria to the clinic and get back here before Noah arrived.

They couldn't go out now that she'd lost her babysitter, but maybe she could invite him in for a game of Hungry Hungry Hippos with the kids.

Give her a break for a while.

On a new mission, she pulled on the jeans and white T-shirt she'd discarded earlier and hurried back to the living room.

"Is Luke on his way?"

"Yes. He said not to have the baby without him." Victoria gripped her stomach as another contraction hit.

Lindsay couldn't be sure, but she thought the contractions were coming closer together. "Well, that's the fun part about babies. They come on their own time."

Grabbing her flip-flops, she called down the hall. "Kids! We have to go."

Melissa opened her bedroom door as Caleb and Jacob came out into the hall in their pajamas. "Where're we going?"

"To take Victoria to the clinic."

"I'm watching reruns of *Gossip Girl*. We were both supposed to watch the marathon together," Melissa said accusingly.

Melissa's ability to make her feel guilty had grown exponentially over the past few weeks. While she desperately tried to find time for her, it was challenging with four other children demanding her attention. "I'm sorry Mel, it slipped my mind."

"Whatever." She went back inside her room and shut the door.

Seriously? "Mel, come on. I'm not kidding."

She knew putting that extra TV in the girl's room had been a mistake. How many times had Rachel and Nathan told her no? She glanced toward the ceiling. *Would a guidebook to raising your children have been too much to ask for?*

Melissa's stare-down when she opened the door was intense, but Lindsay was having none of it.

"I invented that look. Go get your shoes or you'll be getting a personal view of how babies are born."

Behind her, Jacob's eyes widened. "Aunt Vic's having her baby?"

"Now?" Caleb asked, rushing into the living room.

Someone was going to be a gynecologist. Of course—med school. No problem. Lindsay sighed, immediately distracted by Victoria's cry.

Melissa's frown faded as she rushed to get her shoes.

"Lindsay!"

She stopped at the door to the babies' room and headed back to the living room.

Victoria was shaking her head. "You know what, I'm not doing this." She struggled to get up from the couch and Lindsay extended a hand to help. "I'm not having a baby. In fact, I'm going back to New York. Climbing the corporate ladder wasn't so bad."

"Vic…" She'd seen this before. At the point of no return, many women decided they'd changed their minds about what was about to happen.

Victoria would get through it as everyone else did and, in a few hours…or maybe eight or nine, she'd be happier than she'd ever imagined possible. Until, of course, the kid learned to talk back.

"Mel!"

"Right here," she said from directly behind her.

"Oh. Please help support Aunt Vic on the other side," she said.

The three of them hobbled toward the door and Lindsay opened it, ushering Victoria outside.

"Seriously, Lindsay, I can't do this." Victoria's eyes widened as another wave of pain hit.

Definitely closer to baby time.

"Yes, you can. Melissa, help her to the minivan and I'll go get your sisters." She turned to Victoria. "Just hang in there. I'm going to get you to the clinic and Dr. McCarthy will take care of you."

"No."

"They have drugs—strong ones. The

faster you get there, the faster the pain will stop."

Victoria began to waddle with determination toward the van.

"Thought so," Lindsay said as Noah's motorcycle pulled into her driveway.

Great, he was early.

Then a thought hit her. Great, he was early! He could stay with the children.

"Kids, out of the van. Go back inside," she said.

Melissa jutted her lip out. "I thought you said—"

"For once, Mel, don't argue," she replied, turning to Noah. "Thank God you're early." She hugged him quickly.

"I would have been here at noon if I'd known I'd get that kind of reaction." He set his helmet on the bike and unzipped his leather jacket.

The smell of his manly aftershave shook her for a second. "Yeah, date's off."

He shook his head. "No way. I told you—"

"Shh." She swatted his arm. "Victoria's in labor. I'm taking her to the clinic. I need you to watch the kids for, like, twenty minutes," she said quickly, dragging him toward the house.

"Seriously?"

"Yes."

"This isn't another excuse—"

"Lindsay! Hurry the hell up!" Victoria yelled from inside the van.

Noah's eyes widened. "Okay, so what do I do with the kids?"

"You're asking the wrong person," she mumbled. "The babies are asleep, just keep the other three occupied for half an hour."

"Whoa. You said twenty minutes."

She pushed him inside. "I'll be back soon."

She didn't have time to even question her decision about leaving the kids with Noah as she raced to the minivan and climbed in. She leaned across and buckled Victoria's seat belt for the fast drive to the clinic six blocks away. "Okay, let's go," she said, putting the van in Reverse.

"What if I can't do this? I mean, physically can't." Victoria sounded terrified.

Of all the people...of all the situations. How on earth was *she* Victoria Mason's support system right now? Life was dishing out far too much irony these days.

"You can and you will. One way or the other, this baby is coming out, so I need you to be strong, okay."

To her surprise, Victoria reached across and grabbed her hand on the wheel. "Will you stay with me?"

Really?

"I'm actually not working, so technically..."

"Please, Lindsay. Rachel was supposed to be here with me, in case Luke couldn't make it."

"Fine. Until Luke gets here."

Sorry, Noah.

FIVE KIDS. NO PROBLEM. He could handle this. Not that the panicking blondes had left him much choice. At least the babies were asleep. That made things a little easier.

In the living room, Jacob and Caleb were watching cartoons. A purple monkey in red boots blew out candles on a birthday cake.

"Hey, guys, what are you watching?"

"Dora," Jacob said, his eyes glued to the set.

"Dora's the monkey?"

"No, Noah. Dora is the girl. The monkey is Boots."

"The monkey's name is Boots?"

"Yes. Because he wears red boots all the time," Caleb explained.

He scanned the living room. Toys littered the floor and coloring sheets with crayons covered the coffee table. On the couch, a load of laundry sat waiting to be folded and on the end table, a coffee cup and wineglass sat next to a rocking chair.

Obviously the place Lindsay started and ended her day.

And despite how worn out she must be, she'd agreed to go out with him.

"Where's Melissa?"

"In her room," Jacob said as the cartoon's ending theme song started to play.

"Which one is hers?" Noah asked, standing.

"The last one, next to the bathroom," Jacob said as another episode of the same show started.

Noah walked down the hall and tapped on the bedroom door. "Melissa, it's Noah."

No answer.

"Aunt Lindsay should be back soon."

"I don't care," came the reply.

Okey-dokey.

His cell phone signaled a new text message.

So sorry, but I'm going to be a little longer than planned. Can you handle things for a bit longer?

He wanted to help her, to be here for her, for whatever she needed.

This was what she needed.

I got this. Take your time, he texted back.

Tapping on Melissa's door again, he said, "Did you want to come watch—" what were the boys watching again? "—some cartoon about a monkey in boots with us?"

"No."

Of course not. She was almost nine.

"Do you want something to eat?"

"No."

Wow, Lindsay hadn't been kidding about the child's unwillingness to leave her bedroom. They couldn't keep taking doors off hinges. At some point she had to open up and talk to them.

"Okay, well, the boys and I are going to order pizza. I'll let you know when it arrives." What kid could resist pizza?

No answer.

He pulled out his cell phone and hit the speed-dial button for the small pizza shop just outside of town. They didn't normally deliver this far out, but he'd gotten one of his at-risk kids a job doing deliveries for the company the month before, so he knew he could pull some strings.

The doorbell rang almost exactly as the pizzeria answered and Noah had to hang up to go open the door.

A tall, dark-haired man stood on the porch, his back to him.

"Hello?"

The guy turned and frowned.

Lindsay, tell me you didn't double book yourself for two dates tonight.

"I was looking for Lindsay," the man said, leaning back to glance at the number on the house.

"This is her house. Who are you?" Noah asked, blocking the entryway. If she had double booked herself, she couldn't have picked more different men. In a pair of dark gray pants and a white dress shirt, open at the collar, the guy looked as if he'd stepped from the pages of a men's catalog.

"A friend. Who are you?"

"Likewise."

The stare-down was intense between them until finally the other man asked, "Well, is she here?"

"No. She had to go to work." It was sort of true.

"Oh. And you're...babysitting?"

Whoever it was knew enough about Lindsay's current situation. "Yes. I'm Noah," he said reluctantly, hoping to get a name out of this guy. He couldn't remember seeing him around town before.

"Ben Walker."

The children's godfather. Nathan's business partner. A man Lindsay had dated.

The guy who'd hung up on her and hadn't bothered to show up for the funeral.

Noah's eyes narrowed. "I'll let her know you stopped by," he said coldly.

"Noah, is that the pizza already?" Caleb asked, coming up behind him in the doorway.

"Uh, no…"

The boy's eyes widened. "Hey! Uncle Ben!"

Fantastic.

Ben smiled. "Hi, Jake!"

"Caleb," the boy corrected, stepping past Noah.

"I knew that."

Lie. No one knew that. The boys were virtually identical.

"Did you bring us any new video games?" Caleb asked, hugging him and glancing up eagerly.

"As a matter of fact, I did," Ben said.

"Come in!" The little boy took the guy's hand.

Noah moved away from the door. "Sure, come in," he muttered.

"Jacob, look who's here…and he brought new video games," Caleb said, dragging Ben into the living room.

Jacob jumped up and ran for a hug.

An unexplainable tug wrenched at Noah's chest. He may not know this guy, but clearly the kids were happy to see him. Would Lindsay be?

He clenched his teeth as the guy ruffled

Jacob's hair. "Hey, buddy, is this the episode where they help save the pirates?" he asked, nodding toward the television.

"The monkey's name is Boots," he said before he could stop himself.

Ben grinned over his shoulder. "Yeah, I got that." He scanned the room. "Where are your sisters?"

"Abby and Mac are asleep and Mel won't come out of her room since…" Jacob's gaze dropped.

Ben knelt in front of him. "It's okay, buddy. I'm sorry I wasn't here sooner, but I'm here now. Everything's going to be okay."

And despite Noah's best efforts, he could no longer be annoyed at the man. The boys had showed more signs of life in the past three minutes than they had in a month from what he'd gathered. Maybe this guy being here wasn't such a bad thing.

At least not for Lindsay and the boys.

"I checked on her, but she doesn't want to come out. Maybe once the pizza arrives," Noah said, not sure what to do next.

Was Ben planning to stay until Lindsay

got home? If so, should he leave? Stay? He didn't know this guy...the kids seemed to...

"I can get her to come out," Ben said, moving past him into the hall.

Really? He'd like to see him try. So far, nothing had worked.

"Which door?" Ben asked from the end of the hall.

Noah pointed to it and then leaned against the wall to watch.

"Mel, it's Ben."

Nothing.

Noah couldn't help feeling slightly satisfied. "See?"

Ben nodded. "Mel, if you don't want to come out, that's totally cool...but the boys and I were about to watch *Frozen*."

The bedroom door swung open. "You brought *Frozen*?" she asked, wiping her cheeks quickly.

Noah's mouth gaped.

"Yep," Ben said, opening his arms for a hug.

Okay, he may have been able to get Mel to open the door but...

The girl rushed into his arms. "I'm so glad you're here, Uncle Ben," she whispered.

Okay, then.

The two came down the hall toward him and he forced a smile at Mel. "Hi."

"Is the pizza here?" she asked.

"I'll order it right away," he said, reaching for his phone, but Ben stopped him.

"Now that I'm here, you don't have to stay. I can take it from here."

Noah hesitated. By the look of things, Ben had things under control for the first time since the kids' parents had died. "I told Lindsay I'd take care of them."

"Trust me, it's fine. She'll be happy I'm here."

That's what Noah was afraid of.

CHAPTER SEVEN

THE SIGHT OF Ben's Land Rover parked next to Noah's motorcycle in her driveway made Lindsay's heart race. So, he'd finally decided to show up. Not exactly good timing.

Parking the minivan behind the luxurious vehicle she'd admittedly found impressive on their date, she grabbed her purse and hopped down.

As she walked up the pathway, she noticed Noah sitting on the porch step. "Hi," she said, stopping in front of him.

"Hi."

"So, um, I'm guessing Ben's here." She toyed with her keys.

"That's one fantastic ride he has. The man has good taste." His gaze held hers and she blushed.

"I'll admit, I was tempted to key it on my way past."

"I still might," he said as he stood.

She smiled. He was jealous. She wasn't hating that.

"I wasn't sure if you'd have wanted me to leave but, uh…"

"I'm glad you stayed." She knew the kids were okay with Ben, but the fact Noah hadn't bailed the moment he was free to go was a relief.

"They just finished watching *Frozen*. Apparently that was the key to getting Mel to come out of her room." He shoved his hands into his jeans' pockets and descended the steps.

"Melissa is out of her bedroom?"

He nodded.

"That's great. Thank you."

"It was all Ben."

She bit her bottom lip, not sure what to say. "Well…"

"Yeah. Right. I should go." He paused. "By the way, how's Vic?"

"Harper was born twenty minutes ago. Luke made it just in time," she said, covering a yawn with her hand. As she did, she noticed the faint fingernail marks from Victoria's maniacal grip.

She'd been fortunate Luke had arrived before the worst of it.

"Harper?"

"Yeah, in honor of Rachel and Nathan. A girl." The name had surprised her and there hadn't been a dry eye in the room.

"It's nice. Anyway, you should probably get inside." Moving past her, he gave her shoulder a squeeze.

"Noah, I'm sorry about tonight," she said to his back.

He put on his helmet. "Don't sweat it, Lindsay. I'm not giving up."

CLOSING THE DOOR to the babies' room ten minutes later, she tiptoed down the hallway to the kitchen, looking into Mel's and the boys' rooms as she passed. All asleep. Amazing. She hadn't gotten them all to sleep before ten o'clock once that month.

Pausing in the doorway, she took a deep breath before walking through. "So, what are you doing here?" she asked Ben.

He cleared his throat and shifted in his chair. "I spoke to your parents…"

She glared. Her mother had been leaving

her voice mails for over a week, asking if she'd reconsidered her decision regarding the kids, and she'd yet to return a single call. If she thought sending Ben here to talk sense into her would work…

But he continued quickly before she could say anything. "I should have been here weeks ago." He glanced at the coffee cup in his hand. "I'm sorry, Lindsay. I was in shock when you called that day."

"We all were." She wasn't about to let him off the hook. According to Noah, the kids were responding and interacting with him. For the first time in weeks they were laughing and having fun. Something no one else had been able to do for them. Obviously, he was good for them, and that made her angrier he hadn't been here sooner.

The least he could have done was call the children, instead of her parents.

He set the cup aside and stood. "That wasn't a good enough reason to stay away. I don't blame you for being upset." He hugged her while her arms remained stiff by her sides.

"You still haven't told me why you're here now."

He took a step back. "I'm here to help."

"I don't need your help."

"I got Melissa to come out of her room. That has to count for something, right?" He bent to look into her eyes, his six-foot-two frame putting him almost a foot taller.

She turned her head away from his hopeful expression. "The Disney movie did that, not you."

She wasn't about to let him call himself a hero for showing up late and bribing the kids. She'd been the one making all the tough decisions. Or not making them, as the case may be.

He nodded slowly. "Okay. Look, I know I screwed up by not being here right away. For the funeral. The truth is," he said quietly, "I was angry."

She frowned. "Angry?"

What did he have to be angry about? She was the one who'd had to get up every morning, despite a weight pressing against her chest and eyelids that wanted nothing more than to stay closed, to plan a funeral for the two people in her life she'd always depended on to be there. Two people the children depended on.

"Nathan and Rachel were like family to me. Even though I lived in Newark, I was closer to them than anyone else."

He paused and swallowed hard.

"He was a good man. They were a terrific couple and the kids…" Placing his hands on his hips, he looked away.

The annoyance she felt for him faded a little as she watched him struggle to regain control over the emotions overwhelming him.

"I was angry I'd lost not only my business partner, but my best friend. And I was terrified." He sat in a chair and sank against the wooden back. "I had no idea how to see the kids." He studied his hands in silence.

"Well, you did all right," she said with a sigh. They'd all been through the ringer, and people dealt with grief in their own way. His actions may not have been noble, but they were real and she couldn't continue to fault him for his pain.

She sat across from him and kicked off her flip-flops, tucking her legs under her.

"How long do you plan to stay?"

"As long as you'll have me."

"What about work?"

"Nathan was able to work from here. I can, too," he said, but he sounded non-committal.

"Well, the B and B is closed. They shut down for a few weeks following the funeral…and now that Vic has had the baby, I'm not sure what they plan to do."

"If it's okay with you, I can stay here. It would be easier to help out with the kids."

She thought of Noah and the look on his face that evening. He wouldn't be okay with this, but did he really have a say?

The truth was, it would be a big help to have someone here full-time to help with the kids…at least until they all adjusted. Besides, the kids were responding best to Ben and she was sure they would want him to stay.

"You know what," Ben said, standing and reaching for his keys on the counter, "that's probably not a good idea. I mean, Noah…"

"There's nothing going on between Noah and me," she said. Even though it was true, she felt guilty.

Ben smiled. "I'm not going to lie and say I'm sorry to hear that. Maybe this isn't the best timing, but it's good to see you. I wanted to apologize for being such a jerk that night at dinner."

She waved a dismissive hand. "That seems like a million years ago."

"Even so, I am sorry. At the time, Nate and I were arguing over a big account." He paused. "But I'm here now, one hundred percent."

This was one more complication she had no idea how to handle. She sighed and looked down.

"You okay?"

"Yeah…no…I don't know. I just don't get why they left the kids to us. I mean, they could have chosen Leigh. She would have been a fantastic choice. Or even Victoria and Luke would have made more sense." She paused. "It's not that I don't want to take care of the kids, I do. I worry about them.

I wish Nathan and Rachel had had a better backup plan, that's all."

Ben moved to stand behind her and began to massage her shoulders. "They must have had their reasons."

Lindsay tensed then turned to face him. "Well, it would have been great to have shared them with us."

Her brother had never approved of her and her choices, so why he would leave the futures of his five children in her hands was baffling. He had to have known she'd mess this up somehow...probably often. Okay, all the freaking time.

"Well, what did it say in your letter?" Ben asked.

She frowned. "What letter?"

"The one from the lawyer who drafted their will." He looked confused.

"You got a letter?" Anger and hurt competed for her top emotion. "I didn't," she said quietly.

Ben knelt in front of her. "Again, I'm sorry. I thought—"

"It's okay. My brother and I weren't exactly close." She shrugged.

He'd left Ben a letter explaining his decision, but not her?

She fought the overwhelming desire to ask if his letter had at least mentioned her. Instead, she straightened. "The kids have all my spare rooms, so you're on the couch. I'll go get you some blankets."

"Lindsay."

She stopped.

"I'm sure he had his reasons."

Maybe, but now she'd never know what they were.

"I CAN'T BELIEVE you were able to convince her to go to summer camp," Lindsay said the next morning as she poured coffee for her and Ben.

After the epic battle she'd had with Melissa the day before about the eight-week summer program Rachel had signed her up for, she'd thought for sure she'd have to try to come up with alternative arrangements for her that summer while she was at the clinic.

But once again, Ben had worked his magic. He'd crashed on the sofa the night before, and though she'd been hesitant to let him stay, his help at 3:00 a.m. with Mackenzie and Abigail had certainly been appreciated. She'd always marveled over Rachel's ability to make parenting two sets of twins and a fifth child look easy, but never so much as these past few weeks.

"I reminded her about the bike Nathan had promised for her birthday this year." He opened the fridge door and took out a carton of milk.

"He promised her a bike?"

Her suddenly stretched finances couldn't afford one right now. She'd converted the couples' life insurance policy into a bank account to help raise the children—her nurse's salary certainly couldn't handle that pressure—but she wasn't sure how far that money would go. The cost of adopting her nieces and nephews had never crossed her mind until now when she was considering buying more family-friendly furniture. Her white leather was already showing signs of abuse. Better to sell it while it was still in good shape.

"Don't worry," Ben said, reading her mind. "I ordered it from Play Hard."

"You did?"

"This morning after she agreed to go to summer camp."

Lindsay wasn't sure what to say. "Thank you," she croaked out as the three oldest kids walked into the kitchen.

After their 3:00 a.m. wakeup, the babies were sleeping in a little longer than usual.

"Hi, guys. What kind of cereal do you want?" She opened the pantry, displaying the selection of individual-size cereal boxes she'd stocked up on the week before. She didn't eat breakfast, coffee being her major source of fuel, so the kids were quickly learning the homemade breakfasts they'd grown accustomed to at the B and B were a thing of the past.

"Cereal again?" Melissa pouted as she sat at the table.

"Next week I'll try to start cooking when we have more time," Lindsay said, feeling her cheeks grow hot under Ben's gaze.

Let him judge her lack of culinary and

parenting skills, she didn't care. She'd never once claimed to be good at this.

"Fine," Melissa grumbled. "Froot Loops, please."

Lindsay took three bowls out of the cupboard and started opening the cereal. Most mornings, she'd added the milk to the boxes, but she wanted to look as though she was at least trying to make an effort. Because she was.

"We're eating out of bowls?" Jacob asked, his eyes wide.

"Yes," Lindsay said, setting the bowls in front of them on the table and diving for her coffee. She took a gulp. It burned her tongue.

Ben nodded toward Melissa. "She's not planning to leave the house wearing that, is she?" he whispered.

Lindsay scanned her niece's outfit. Jean shorts and a T-shirt. She shrugged. "She's going to summer camp. What's the problem?"

"The pockets of the shorts hang down beyond the edge of the denim," Ben said, as if she were blind not to have noticed.

The truth was she was fairly certain she'd been the one to help her niece cut her old jeans that way. She owned a similar pair. "Oh…yeah. Right. I'll ask her to change." Though she really wasn't getting his problem. It was summer. It was hot. The girl was eight.

"Ask?" Ben's eyebrows raised.

"Tell?"

He nodded with a small laugh. "I'll shower then drop the kids off at camp." He tossed his remaining coffee into the sink and she almost dove after it. Coffee was never wasted around here.

"Really?"

"Yeah, really. I meant what I said, I'm here to help."

With that, he left the kitchen, leaving her to deal with Melissa's choice of wardrobe; a battle she wasn't sure she was on the right side of anymore.

"OKAY. NOW, THIS is simple…put your foot on the clutch and give it a little gas." Noah watched as Dominic nervously threw his leg over the side of the motorcycle.

"I don't know, Noah."

"What are you talking about? For a year you've been begging me to teach you how to ride my bike."

"I never actually thought you'd let me."

Neither had he. "A promise is a promise. Now, put on the helmet," he said, handing him his spare.

Dominic wrinkled his nose. "It smells like perfume."

"Yeah, not many dudes ride behind me on this thing."

Correction: no dude had ever ridden behind him on his bike. He'd been hoping it would smell like a particular pretty blonde after last night. He still couldn't believe the events of the night before, even though they'd weighed heavily on him all night.

Lindsay had finally agreed to go out and then Victoria goes into labor.

He might have found it funny if Ben hadn't then showed up.

Now he had no idea if he'd get the chance again.

The fact that he'd been completely out of his element with the younger kids hadn't escaped him. Older teens he could handle, even help. Young kids were a different breed.

Ben hadn't had any trouble at all.

Dominic sighed and put on the helmet. "I'm ready."

"Start slow. Put your foot on the clutch and give it a little gas. Just a little."

Dominic did, and the bike roared and lurched forward. He stopped in a panic. "That's it. I'm done." He started to remove the helmet, but Noah stopped him.

"Stay on," he grumbled, tossing a leg over the back to sit behind him. "I can't believe I'm doing this," he muttered under his breath.

As he reached around the kid to start the bike, a Land Rover pulled up in front of the community center.

Ben. Just great.

"Wow, now *that's* a sweet ride," Dominic said.

"Hey, do you want to learn to drive this or not?" Noah snapped. "Okay, foot on clutch." His gaze was glued to the Land Rover.

Melissa, Jacob and Caleb climbed out of

the back with their backpacks and lunch
bags. They must be here for the summer
camp program. Ben was dropping them off?
Did that mean he'd stayed at Lindsay's the
night before? And she was letting him help
with the kids.

He turned the handle roughly, giving it
too much gas and, as the bike flew forward
across the parking lot, he had to grip Dominic to steady himself from flying off the
back. He hit the brake and they both flew
forward.

"Who's teaching who how to drive?" Ben
said as he passed, a smirk on his face.

"Hi, Noah!" Jacob and Caleb waved.

"Hey, guys. Hi, Melissa," he said, shutting off the bike.

She nodded.

"Glad to see you all made it for summer
camp. Where's your aunt?" He climbed off
the bike.

"Linds was running late this morning,
Ben said. "We stayed up…chatting…last
night."

Linds? Noah felt his chest tighten. So the
guy had stayed at her place.

"I offered to drop the kids off today."

He nodded. "Well, I'll be around most of the day, so I can drive them home later, save you the trouble of coming back."

Ben glanced at the bike. "On that?"

Right. What was he going to do, take them one at a time? But he sure didn't want the jerk to win this one.

"Actually, no. I thought I'd give them a ride in the fire truck," he said, winking at the kids. Ethan, the head of the fire squad owed him one from the MMA fight tickets he'd scored him a few months before.

Please don't let there be an emergency in Brookhollow at five o'clock today.

The boys' faces lit up. "Can we, Ben?" they asked.

Noah could see the guy's jaw clench. "Sure. You bet." He ruffled the boys' hair and handed Melissa her backpack. "You guys go on in. Have a great first day."

The two of them watched as the kids signed in with one of the camp counselors.

When they were inside, Ben turned to Noah. "Look, I see what you're doing—"

"What *I'm* doing? Come on! It took you

weeks to get here and now you're trying to look like a hero?"

Ben took a step toward him and placed a hand on his shoulder. "All I'm saying is... I've got it from here."

"ARE YOU SURE you can do this?" Lindsay asked Leigh later that morning, but she knew the answer. Leigh would never say no to helping with the girls, even if they weren't Rachel's children. Her home was always open to children and there was no one Lindsay trusted more than the caring day-care worker and her staff.

"Of course," she said. "These precious little angels are welcome here anytime," she said as Lindsay set Mackenzie in a high chair next to her sister.

Precious little angels? Lindsay yawned. "More like precious little sleep-destroyers. 3:00 a.m., like clockwork, they're awake." She yawned again. "Every night."

"Try waking them up for a pull-up change before you go to bed," Logan said, appearing in the kitchen, a box under his arm.

"How will that work?" She was afraid if

she woke them around midnight before she went to bed, they'd never settle down again.

"Well, it's probably because they're wet that they wake up, right?"

"Yes."

"So if you wake them, bring them to the potty, then put them down with a fresh pull-up, I'd bet they'd sleep until morning."

Lindsay glanced between Leigh and Logan. "Tell me the truth. Did you two receive some secret parenting book when you adopted Olivia that the rest of us don't know about? I'd pay any amount for a copy."

"We've been doing it longer, is all," Logan said, kissing his nine-year-old daughter Amelia on the head.

"Are those your new books, Dad?" Amelia asked, nodding toward the box he carried.

Leigh's eyes widened, but Logan shook his head. "I'll show you later."

"I want to see," Lindsay said. "How often does one get parenting advice and a sneak peek at a best-selling author's new book? Come on, open the box."

Leigh shrugged and Logan sighed, but he set the box on the counter and opened it.

The four of them peered inside.

Lindsay frowned as she read the title, *The Promise of Love* by Leigh Logan? She glanced at Leigh, her eyes wide. "You two are co-writing romance novels now?" Amazing.

"No!" Leigh shook her head. "Not really. Logan does all the writing. I'm more like the inspiration."

Their nine-year-old pushed her breakfast away. "Gross."

Lindsay reached into the box. "I'm taking one of these."

"You can't tell anyone," both Leigh and Logan said in unison.

"Of all people, you two should know nothing around here stays secret for long," Lindsay said, tucking the novel into her purse and kissing the two girls. "Besides, this is the best bit of gossip I've had to share all year."

THE SOUND OF a fire-truck siren echoed through her living room walls later that day and she rushed to the window, glancing toward Victoria and Luke's house.

She released a sigh of relief when she saw the house looked fine—no flames, no smoke—and she couldn't hear the smoke detector as she normally could when Victoria tried to cook.

When the truck pulled into her driveway instead, she narrowed her eyes to look through the windshield. Noah? She went to the door and opened it as three kids hopped down from the truck with Noah's help.

Oh, he was wearing his firefighter's uniform. That was hardly fair. A man's hotness rating went up by at least ten points when he wore a uniform of any kind. Military, police, fireman—it didn't matter. And Noah had nowhere else to go on the hotness scale.

"Hey, what's going on?" she asked, stepping outside.

"Aunt Lindsay, that was the coolest thing ever!" Jacob said, dragging his backpack on the ground.

"Yeah, it was totally awesome," Caleb agreed. "Noah let us run the siren all the way from the community center."

"Yes, I heard it," she said with a laugh. "I thought Vic was trying to cook again."

He laughed as he lifted Melissa from the truck.

"Hey, Mel, how was summer camp?"

The girl had a dreamy expression as she said, "I'm in love."

What was the appropriate reaction to that? On one hand, as cool Aunt Lindsay, she was amused and happy for the kid, especially since she was finally happy. On the other, as a responsible guardian, she was nervous.

Nathan had forbidden his child to date until she was twenty-five, and while she'd thought it extreme before, she was starting to see her brother's side.

"Really? On the first day?"

"It's love at first sight. Like mom and dad."

She caught her breath. Since the day of the funeral, that was the first time Melissa had mentioned her parents.

"Well, it certainly was for them, so who knows?" She caressed the girl's cheek.

"Can I call him?"

Lindsay hesitated. "You have his number?"

She nodded.

Lindsay looked helplessly at Noah.

He shrugged, clearly as confused as she felt.

"Five minutes, okay?"

"Okay," the girl said, hugging her. "Thanks, Aunt Lindsay."

When the kids disappeared inside, she said, "Love at first sight at eight."

"Oh, come on, you know you had a boyfriend in fourth grade."

"Yes, exactly. That's what I'm worried about." She bit her lip.

"You turned out okay," he said.

"The jury's still out on that."

"I'm making the ruling and I say you're perfect."

She swallowed hard. "So, why are you dropping off the kids?"

Had Ben forgotten to pick them up? She wanted to be angry, but she'd actually forgotten a few times. It wasn't easy for non-parents to think like parents.

She sometimes still forgot to bathe the

kids every night, the way Rachel used to. And the last thing she wanted was to be known as the aunt who sent smelly kids to camp.

"I offered to drive them when I saw Ben drop them off this morning."

She winced. His tone sounded nonchalant, light, but she knew he was probably dying to know what had happened between her and Ben.

"Things are complicated. He's helping."

She shoved her hands into her jeans' pockets and rocked back on her heels.

"You don't owe me an explanation."

Then why did she feel as though she did? "Did you want to come in…for a drink or something?"

"I would, but I have to get the truck back in case there's an emergency. Besides, I don't drink while I'm training."

Training. Right. His fight was less than two weeks away.

"How's that going?" she asked in an attempt not to reveal her discomfort on the subject.

"Good. Brandon finally let me back in the gym." He laughed, shaking his head.

"That's...great."

"You don't really think so."

"Well, it doesn't matter what I think."

"It does to me," he said, moving closer and reaching for her. "Come to the fight."

She shook her head.

He wrapped his arms around her waist and pulled her close. "Okay."

Her pulse raced as his hold tightened around her and he stroked her cheek. She felt so tiny in his big arms. Tiny and safe and...happy.

When he lowered his lips to hers, she felt her knees give way beneath her. She gripped the back of his firefighter's jacket as he leaned down to look at her.

"Fighting's not your thing. I respect that."

But fighting was his thing.

"How about breakfast tomorrow?"

He pulled back and looked at her in surprise. "You're asking *me* out?"

There was no harm in that, right? She owed him for canceling their night out. And the whole Ben thing had her feeling as if she owed him something.

She sighed. "Answer quickly before I change my mind."

"Yes. Breakfast. I love breakfast."

CHAPTER EIGHT

"FINALLY," NOAH SAID, leaning back in his chair under the umbrella of the outside tables at Joey's Diner on Main Street.

Lindsay raised an eyebrow over the coffee cup she'd been clinging to as if it were a life preserver since she'd met him for the breakfast thing. "Does it really count if I can barely keep my eyes open?"

"I'm sorry. The thing is…you shocked me when you asked and I had forgotten about previous commitments I have today. But I desperately wanted this…breakfast."

"We could have rescheduled."

"You wouldn't have," he said matter-of-factly. "I was forced to come to your house and drag your butt out of bed."

The look on Ben's face when he'd arrived that morning had made it all the more sweet.

"You're probably right," she said, smiling over her coffee cup.

Man, even sleepy and grumpy, he couldn't resist touching her. Leaning forward, he reached across the table and, taking her cup from her, set it aside and took both of her small hands in his.

"I'm not sure how soon we can see each other again after this morning. I'm training all week and then Friday I head to Newark for the fight weigh-ins that afternoon. The fight's Saturday, followed by post-fight conferences."

Her expression fell, but to her credit she hid her disappointment well.

"That's fine. I've got a lot going on this week, too. In fact, I've got a lot going on forever. Or at least for the next sixteen years. What's the legal age that you can kick children out of the house?"

"I think the day after Mac and Abby turn eighteen, you should be in the clear," he said with a sympathetic laugh. Her life really had been altered drastically and he marveled over her ability to adjust as well as she had.

He wondered how much of that had to do with Ben and he fought a feeling of jealousy and annoyance that it was the other man helping her with the children. He wanted to be the one she could rely on.

The waiter approached with the coffee pot and Lindsay nodded, extending her nearly empty cup.

"I can't believe you're not constantly vibrating with all the coffee you drink," he said.

She smiled as she cradled the fresh refill between both hands. "I can't believe you don't drink coffee. How do you stay awake?"

"My secret," he said with a wink.

"So, today…your plans? More fight preparation?"

He took a sip of orange juice and hesitated. "I promised someone I would help them with something."

"Family stuff?"

Dominic was probably the closest to family he had, so he nodded. "Sort of." He paused and when she remained silent, he knew what she was thinking.

"Come with me."

Dominic wouldn't mind Lindsay hanging out with them today. And Noah certainly wasn't looking forward to leaving her, especially if this was their only chance to be together this week.

"I don't know, Noah. Meeting the parents is really not my thing. I never know what to say or how to act."

She looked panicked.

"My mom left my dad and me when I was seven and I haven't seen her since. My dad and I haven't spoken in over ten years—he's an alcoholic and not a nice man," he confided for the first time.

"I didn't know that. I'm sorry, Noah."

The last time he'd seen his father was the day he'd come home from juvenile detention only to find him drunk, no food in the house and the place a mess.

When his father had swung at him, he'd countered with moves he'd learned from some of the other boys in the center. It would surprise most people to know juvie had been the place he'd felt safe and cared for, and hadn't had to wonder where his next meal would come from.

She stroked the palm of his hand with her

thumb. "So if we're not meeting your parents, who are we going to see?"

He smiled. "You'll see."

LINDSAY COULDN'T REMEMBER a time she'd ever felt as content, as carefree or as excited than she was at this moment, on the back of Noah's motorcycle, her arms wrapped tightly around his waist.

Noah's confession about his family made her ache for him... For a mother to leave her child behind to deal with an alcoholic father alone... That was unacceptable—no matter the circumstance.

As a nurse she felt as though she was helping people and she could offer love and support and assistance during difficult times for them and their families. It was a different kind of heartache. But one she could handle.

He turned into the community-center parking lot and stopped near the back entrance.

He removed his helmet and climbed off, helping her to do the same. "The community center?"

"Yeah. There are some pretty cool kids here I'd like you to meet."

"Noah, if you have a kid, tell me quickly." She'd dated single dads before and she was okay with men who had children...who were divorced...but a heads-up was always nice. Being blindsided by a child or worse, an ex-wife, was not something she was okay with.

He shook his head. "Lindsay, take a breath. No kid...or ex-wife, in case you were wondering. Don't you think I might have mentioned something before now?"

His amusement made her laugh.

"Sorry, I've dated a lot of men with disclosure issues," she muttered.

"Come on." Taking her hand, he headed toward the door.

Noticing some teenage boys near the building smoking and eyeing the bike, she said, "Um, Noah, are you sure your bike is okay?"

"Don't worry, they always bring it back," he said, opening the door and holding it for her.

Inside tables were set up and kids studied

in small groups. Several older teens played volleyball at the other end of the open room and to their right, another group played cards. She hadn't known the community center offered any programming on weekends. Most of the activities the kids were involved in took place during the week.

"There better not be any betting going on over there," Noah called to the cardplayers.

A nearby kid spoke up. "I've been keeping an eye. Hey, Noah." He turned to look at her with interest.

"Mario, this is my friend, Lindsay. Lindsay, Mario is one of the head volunteers here at Turnaround."

An outreach program? She'd never heard of anything like that in Brookhollow. "Nice to meet you."

"You, too. Are you hoping to get involved?" the high school student asked.

"Um…" She hadn't even known Turnaround existed five minutes ago.

"One thing at a time. I'm introducing her to some of you guys today," Noah said.

"Well, if you want, I can give Lindsay a tour. I think Joanne wanted to talk to you."

The boy frowned. "More denied funding, I think."

Noah's face clouded but, squeezing Lindsay's hand before he released it, he said, "You're in good hands with Mario. This shouldn't take long."

"Oh, yeah, no problem. Go."

As he headed toward the office, she turned her attention to Mario.

"I take it by the look on your face, you didn't even know we existed until now," he said with a smile.

"You caught me. Noah hadn't mentioned where he was taking me," she said.

Noah participated in an at-risk youth outreach program? And he'd never said a word. Most men she'd dated had rarely done an altruistic act in their lives and if they had, they'd have been singing their own praises from the rooftops.

There was clearly a lot more to the man she'd pegged as an empty-headed fighter with a great body.

"Yeah, Noah's not exactly the type of guy to go around announcing that kind of stuff... being a tough MMA fighter and all that," he said with a smirk. "Don't tell him I told you, but he's not that tough."

"Oh, no?"

Mario shook his head. "A softie. He'll do anything for anybody."

His constant offers to help her these past few weeks were proof of that. "He's a great guy. So, how long have you volunteered here with him?"

"Since the first week he started the program, about ten months ago."

Started the program? "You mean the program was his idea?" Lindsay couldn't help but wonder what would have sparked such an interest in Noah. Fighting was the only thing he talked about.

Mario nodded toward the entrance as another boy entered. "There's Dominic. He works with Noah once a week." He waved to the teen.

"Mario, can you help me with my math problems?" a girl of about twelve asked, holding out her summer school math workbook.

The sight of it brought back a million

memories of Lindsay's own summers spent in summer school.

Nathan had always done well in school; the studying had come easy to him, whenever he did study. She'd struggled with a slight learning disability for years and had always had to put in extra time and effort to barely pass her courses.

She hoped Nathan's children had gotten their father's brain.

"Sure." Mario hesitated, glancing at her.

"Go ahead. I'm good," she said.

When the older boy led the girl toward the tables, Lindsay looked around. Several new computers were set up in the space and in the corner next to the indoor basketball nets were several sets of weights where some teenage boys worked out.

She wondered how much of it had been government funded. Probably not much, she thought wryly. Getting government funding for anything, except the local sports programs, was a challenge. Even the medical clinic had to fight for funding and relied heavily on fund-raisers. Like the Fourth of July events in the park next week.

The thought of the Independence Day celebrations made her pause. How would the kids feel about going this year, without their parents? It had been a tradition to go to the fairgrounds together, then stay for the fireworks. This year she was working the medical-clinic booth, and she hoped the kids would be okay with Ben.

Noah came out of the office and she pushed the worry aside.

She cocked her head to the side and tried to look annoyed, but her attempt failed. How could she be upset that he'd never told her about all of this? It was endearing and more than a little fantastic. *He* was endearing and a whole lot of fantastic.

"I GUESS I owe you an explanation," Noah said outside the medical clinic as he was dropping her off for work just before noon.

"You don't owe me anything, but I am curious," she said, taking off the helmet and checking her watch as she climbed off the back of the bike.

"Well, what would you like to know?"

He'd answer anything she asked. Taking

her there had been a big step for him. A discussion about his own past was sure to come up. She was finally softening to the idea of him, and them together, and he was afraid anything she learned about his life before fighting might push her away again. But she had to know everything.

"How did you get involved with the program?"

"It started small. When I met Dominic, I saw a kid who wanted to do the right thing, but he was lost, not sure what the right thing was. I kind of forced my way into his life, offering as much support and encouragement as I could…and then when it seemed to work, I wanted to help more kids."

"Wow."

"It really is wow. These kids could have gone either way, but now they're graduating, some have jobs, and they want to help others. It's great to watch." He smiled.

"You must be really proud."

He nodded.

"Which is why I don't understand why you don't tell anyone about it."

They moved to the picnic table outside the clinic and sat. "The truth is I'm not sure how long the program is going to be able to continue. We keep losing funding because of regulations."

"Regulations," she said in frustration. "I know all about regulations and how they can put such rigid constraints on things to the point of making doing anything good impossible."

Moving closer, he wrapped an arm around her. "The main issue is that I can only be there once a week. I wish I could do more, be here more, be more involved, but with the fighting…"

She stiffened. "Don't you think this is more important than all that?"

Had anything ever been more important than fighting to him? The one thing he knew he was truly good at? The one aspect in his life that had helped him focus his energy and his anger and determination? The thing that had saved him from a less-than-desirable life?

"Lindsay, I know how you feel about

fighting, and I'm not saying you're wrong. It can be brutal. Injuries can be intense. But fighting was *my* Turnaround program."

She turned to look at him again, silent, waiting for him to continue.

"When I was sixteen, I was a mess. With my mom gone and a useless father I couldn't depend on, I got involved with the wrong crowd. At first it was petty stuff—graffiti, breaking into the school after hours, drinking in the park... Then I stole a car."

Her eyes widened and brought him back to his sixteen-year-old self when the judge had looked at him with disappointment in her eyes as she'd sentenced him to a year in juvenile detention.

"When I got out of juvie, things were worse, because at least inside I had consistency. Now, I had nothing."

"Another way the system breaks down," she said quietly.

He nodded. "Anyway, I saw an ad in the paper. The local boxing club was looking for someone to mop the floors after hours, clean the equipment, that sort of thing. And

I didn't want to go back to school…couldn't afford to. So I applied for the job and then Coach Harvey taught me to fight. More than that, he taught me to respect myself and others, and taught me a level of discipline I'd never had before."

She was nodding slowing, but he could tell, she still seemed hesitant to believe any good could come from such an intense, dangerous sport.

"Despite how I feel about fighting, I'm glad you had someone you could trust," she said finally.

"Me, too. It turned my life around. I even went back for my GED a few years later."

She sighed. "I guess I get it…sort of."

He brought her hand to his lips. "I made some mistakes, I bounced back. I'm trying to give these kids the same option. I can't force them to do the right thing, but I can be there for them if they choose to."

"Well, at least you have a plan…and it seems to be working. I have no idea what I'm doing with Nathan's children."

"I think the first step is to start referring to them as yours," he said gently.

"I NEVER WOULD have guessed it," Lily said, taking a bite of her sandwich. She'd stopped by the clinic that evening with dinner and the two sat at the picnic table out back, where she'd sat with Noah just hours before.

The July sun beat down on the concrete, warming her bare feet and, for the first time in months, Lindsay didn't feel stressed.

Ben was taking care of the girls after day care and picking the older children up at summer camp.

"Me, either," she said. "But then, if someone had told me it would happen, I wouldn't have believed anything that's happened to me in the past few weeks."

"So, will you admit you may have misjudged him?"

She sighed. Why did everyone always want to hear they were right? Besides, she still wasn't convinced she was completely wrong about Noah. "You did hear the part about his time in jail?"

Lily rolled her eyes. "Juvenile detention is

hardly jail…besides everyone has skeletons in their closet."

That was true. She was certainly far from perfect. "Fine. He's a good guy."

"Speaking of… How are things with Ben?"

Lindsay groaned. "He's been a godsend. I have no idea what I would have done with the girls this week without him and he's even gotten Melissa to start acting like an eight-year-old instead of a hormonal pre-teen." That was a respite she appreciated for however long they could delay it.

"So?"

"So what?"

"Is there something going on between you two?"

"No," she answered honestly. "Wouldn't it be so much easier if there was?" Why couldn't her heart behave for once and choose the right guy? The guy who had a great job, a great future ahead of him; a guy the children adored.

Instead, it betrayed her at every sight of Noah, every touch from Noah, every thought of Noah.

"What are you going to do? I mean is he

going to stick around and be your room-
mate, take care of the kids while you fall in
love with Noah?"

"Do you think he would? Because that
would be perfect," she said with a wry laugh.

"You have to be fair to him, Lindsay. If
you're never going to be interested in something more with him, you have to tell him."

Her friend was right, but she had no idea
what to do once Ben left. And the kids would
be devastated. "I know. I will." She would…
soon.

EVERYTHING WAS QUIET when she arrived
home later that evening. The smell of chocolate filled the house and, kicking off her
shoes, she followed it to the kitchen, where
a tray of brownies sat on the cooling rack
above the stove. Her stomach growled as
she reached for one, silencing the voice in
her mind that said eating pure sugar at ten
o'clock at night wasn't a good idea.

"I hope that's not the first thing you've
eaten today," Ben said, appearing in the
kitchen with Abby draped over his shoulder.

Lindsay jumped as she turned, but the

sight of the baby girl resting peacefully made the brownie stick in her throat and she coughed. "No…" Cough. "I couldn't resist. Was she having trouble sleeping?" She nodded toward the little girl.

"A bit."

"Sorry I'm so late."

She'd disappeared early that morning with Noah, leaving Ben with the children all day.

"You have to work. It's okay," he said.

Putting the brownie on a napkin, she advanced toward him. "Here, let me put her to bed." The least she could do.

He gently placed the sleeping little girl in her arms.

"I'll be right back. We should talk," she whispered. She couldn't postpone this discussion any longer. Any hope of developing feelings for Ben was vanishing the more time she spent with Noah. Lily was right: she had to tell him that so he could start thinking about his own next steps and how he wanted to move forward with a relationship with the kids.

At least, she assumed he'd want one.

After settling the little girl in her crib

and checking on the other sleeping kids, she changed into a pair of yoga pants and a T-shirt and reluctantly made her way back downstairs.

Ben sat at the kitchen table, a cup of coffee in front of him and one across from him for her. "It's decaf," he said.

She laughed. "A triple espresso wouldn't keep me awake, but thank you." She sat and took a sip. "So, how were the kids today?"

"Great. The boys made pictures for you at summer camp…" He pointed to where they hung on the fridge with alphabet magnets—ones he must have bought because she'd never seen them before now. "And Mel has a new crush."

"Right. Jon?"

"That was yesterday. Today is Gregory."

So much for the reduction in hormones. "Great. Thanks for the update."

The awkward silence between them was so thick she found it suffocating, and the hot coffee made her sweat. She cleared her throat. "Look, Ben, I appreciate your help," she started.

"We make a good team," he said.

"I'm not sure I'm pulling my weight, but thank you for saying that."

"You're doing fine," he said, his tone reserved.

"About Noah this morning…" She stopped, hoping he'd fill in the blanks.

What about Noah? She still hadn't really figured it out herself.

Silence engulfed them until he finally saved her. "I'm not blind…I see that there's something between you two. Something that doesn't exist between us." He paused and she tensed. "But, I'm hoping that could change. I care about you, Lindsay, and I love these kids… I think Nathan and Rachel knew what they were doing when they chose godparents."

She winced. She didn't want to think her brother's matchmaking efforts went beyond the grave. They'd needed to appoint two people and they'd chosen her and Ben; that's as far as that went.

"I'm not sure that was the case, but, either way, I don't want to mislead you. I desperately appreciate your help with the kids, but I don't want you to stay under false pretenses."

"I'm a big boy, Lindsay. If I get hurt at the end of this, then that's a chance I'm willing to take. I told you I'm here to help, and I'm not going to leave you with all of this responsibility."

She swallowed hard. Why couldn't she fall for him? Life would be so much simpler. "Ben, that's sweet, but—"

"Shh. Don't say it. Give me a chance, Lindsay. Give me a chance to win your heart."

She sighed.

All right, Lily, any other great ideas?

CHAPTER NINE

AS IT TURNED OUT, Lily did have another idea about how they could share responsibility of the kids without her giving Ben false hope about where things were going between them.

Based on her work schedule, they'd created a timeshare system for the kids and posted it to the fridge with the new alphabet magnets. Everything for the week was divided between them: pick-ups and drop-offs, meals, bedtimes. They'd also warned the three oldest kids that Ben would be going back to Newark. They'd made sure it was understood that this situation was only temporary until school started again and a different routine could be established.

Lindsay wasn't sure if Ben had completely gotten the message yet, but tonight was his evening for bedtimes, so she enjoyed her rare moment of relaxation. Sort of.

"Ladies, have any of you heard anything I've said?" Bailey asked from her mat at the front of the self-defense class at Extreme Athletics.

Lindsay wasn't sure about the others, but she was certainly having a hard time keeping her eyes from straying across the gym to where Noah and Brandon were training.

In tight-fitting boxers and a T-shirt, the muscles in Noah's thighs and arms strained as he kicked and punched the heavy bag, attacking the leather with an intensity that was both exciting and also a little intimidating.

She couldn't tear her eyes away.

He was so focused she doubted he even knew she was in the room.

"Seriously, ladies. Pay attention. What are you going to do if you get attacked?"

"Hope that Noah's around," Kayla Dawson replied, sitting on her mat to watch the men across the gym.

An overwhelming sense of jealousy overcame Lindsay. Which was ridiculous. It wasn't as if they were a couple.

Who was she kidding? She liked him. A lot. Made even more evident by the fact she'd wanted to see him so badly, she'd attended this tough class of Bailey's.

Bailey sighed as her own gaze drifted across the gym. "He *is* distracting."

"Hey, remember me, Bailey? Your new husband?" Ethan said from his attacker position behind her. He'd been volunteering to act as her assistant since she'd started the Thursday-night class.

"Right. Okay. Eyes to the front, ladies," Bailey said, all business once again.

Lindsay was relieved when Noah winked at her as he packed up and left about twenty minutes later. With him gone, it was definitely easier to learn the defensive techniques. Though what she'd really wanted was to follow him out of the gym.

After the class was over, she lingered.

"Everything okay, Linds?" Bailey asked, sitting on the floor to put on her running shoes.

"Yeah. Hey, Bailey. Can I ask you something?"

"Sure. But if it's something you missed during the class because you were drooling over Noah, then I may refuse to answer."

"How good is he?" She had to know. From what she'd observed of his training, he was quick and on-point...and definitely strong.

"Noah? At fighting, you mean?"

Lindsay nodded, sitting on the corner of Bailey's mat. Over the past few days, his request for her to attend his fight had played over and over in her mind. One minute she thought she could actually do it then her common sense returned.

What if he got hurt? She didn't think she could handle witnessing it firsthand. Tending to his previous injuries had been tough enough when she hadn't seen them occur.

"He's fantastic. His record is six and oh, and four of them have been from submitting some more advanced fighters."

"That's a good thing?"

"Yes. He's undefeated, and for a guy with a boxing background who only started to train MMA seriously last year, he's definitely surprising a lot of people." She paused. "He asked you to go to his fight?"

"Yes."

"Are you going to go?" Bailey stood as Ethan joined them on the mat.

Lindsay stood, as well, feeling her thighs aching already. "I don't think so. I mean I don't think I could handle seeing him get hurt," she said, shaking her head. She cared about him too much to watch him be a punching bag for another fighter.

Ethan looked confused. "Are we talking about Noah?"

"Yes."

"In that case, I think the question you should be asking yourself is how you will feel watching him hurt someone else."

She hadn't even thought of that.

"UH-OH..." ETHAN SAID next to him behind the front desk of the fire hall the next morning.

"What?" Noah asked to his friend's disappearing back as the front door opened and Darlene Dawson walked in.

Oh. *That* uh-oh. He knew why she was here. She'd left three voice mails this week that no one had returned. "Hi, Mrs. D.," he said, silently cursing Ethan. The captain of the fire squad really should be the one to deal with this.

She smiled, and the effect transformed the older woman's face. In her sixties, Mrs. Dawson didn't look a day over forty. Even her light blond, graying hair looked as if it had been dyed that way. Intentional.

"Noah, just the man I was looking for."

He suspected she'd have said that to anyone sitting there. She was on a mission, in her slim-fitting pantsuit and clutching a briefcase. "What can I help you with?"

"Well, as you know, tomorrow is the Fourth of July and as usual we have the fair in town as well as some fund-raising events happening at the park...and I need more volunteers."

She always got straight to the point. He liked that about her.

"Well, I'm not sure who's working that day..." He grinned as he reached for the schedule. "But I'd be happy to give you the names and cell numbers of the guys who aren't."

Her face lit up. "That would be great. And I assume I can count on you, as well?"

Saying no to Mrs. Dawson was near impossible. She was sweet, kind and just slightly flirtatious—and it worked. All the time. "Sure. Where do you need me?"

Opening her briefcase, she pulled out the schedule for the day's events and scanned the list. "I still need a dunkee."

"A what?"

"A dunkee for the dunk tank. It's one of our most popular zones."

"Uh, Mrs. D., do you have anything else I could do?"

He couldn't swim and water wasn't really his thing. Brandon was constantly trying to convince him to add swimming to his workout schedule, claiming the light impact on his joints was safer than running for cardio closer to his fights to prevent injury. But after a close call at the beach in Beach Haven with his father when he was a kid, water had never looked appealing.

"Look, I'll be honest with you. I've had volunteers for that zone, but no one that will—" she eyed his biceps beneath his uniform shirt "—draw a good crowd."

Unbelievable. Now he was eye candy?

He laughed as he shook his head, feeling heat creep across his neck. He could get hit on all day by women, but Mrs. Dawson had a special way of embarrassing him with her compliments.

"I need someone who will encourage the women to step up and spend money to try to dunk them."

"Let me see if some of the other guys can help out. Mark Adams is in great shape and, as an added bonus, he's dated and ticked off almost every woman in town. What better motivation to draw women in?"

She bit her lip. "Good point. But I'll still need one more. I can't expect someone to sit there for ten hours. This zone is so important. It's for the medical clinic and, unfortunately, they depend on these events for funding."

He understood perfectly. His own pleas for funding from the town were repeatedly shot down. "Who's running the medical booth?"

"Lindsay Harper and Melanie Smith."

He didn't hesitate. "I'm in."

The woman eyed him suspiciously. "Thank you...I was expecting more of a fight."

He shrugged. "The clinic is a great cause."

"Well, I guess you do use their services more than most," she said. "And it wouldn't have anything to do with—"

"Nope, nothing at all." He handed her the staff list. "Here you go. As promised, the names and cell numbers."

LINDSAY SAT ACROSS from Mrs. Dawson at Joey's Diner later that day. The fifties-style restaurant on Main Street was the go-to place for meetings, family brunch…just about any get-together in the small town.

"Sorry again about having the girls with me. Ben had work to do today." She wiped ice cream off Abigail's chin at the same time Mackenzie reached for her coffee cup. "Whoa!" She caught the cup just in time.

"No problem, dear." Darlene smiled at the girls. "I've been spending a lot of time at Victoria's helping her with Harper." She lifted Mackenzie from her high chair and set her on her knee. "So, I spoke to Ginger and she said she can deliver to the baked-goods tent by 7:00 a.m. That way Victoria will have plenty of time to get everything unwrapped and displayed on the tables for the sale." She checked her list. "Moving on to your zone—you have everything under control?"

"Yes. We'll use the same tent and demo setup that we used at the May Heart Health Awareness clinic, with the blood-pressure monitoring and the Heart Watch program video."

It wasn't the most exciting booth, but it served as the medic tent and Lost and Found. It was functional, if not fun.

Lindsay scanned the volunteer sheet. "Who do we have in the tank this year?" The mayor would do his customary dunk, where they would raffle off tickets to decide who had a shot at three attempts. Of course, whether the person hit the bull's-eye or not, the lever would be tripped and in he'd go.

"Oh, I forgot to fill in the spaces," Darlene said, handing Lindsay her pen. "It's Mark Adams…"

"Good choice. I wouldn't mind dunking him repeatedly myself," she muttered as she wrote his name on the line. "Who else?"

"Noah Parks."

Her eyes widened. "Noah agreed to do this?"

He was terrified of water. He'd insisted on wearing two life jackets on the boat at Bailey Sheppard's family picnic at their lake house the year before.

"Yes, but only when I told him who'd be running the booth." She eyed her suspiciously. "You wouldn't know why that is, would you?"

Lindsay hid a smile as she shrugged. "No idea."

"THESE LOOK SO GOOD," Lindsay said, eyeing a tray of chocolate peanut-butter cookies inside the B and B tent. "I'd gain ten pounds if I was stationed in this booth today."

"I'm already halfway there." Victoria held up a chocolate-coconut snowball as she continued to stick prices on the trays of desserts. In her yoga shorts and a flowing white tank top, no one would ever guess the woman had recently had a baby.

Her luck never seemed to run out, Lindsay mused.

"Well, Melissa and I thought we'd stop by

to see if you needed any help setting up."
She scanned the tent.

"Actually, somehow I think I managed
to get everything done…" Victoria checked
her watch. "And early. Where are the other
kids?"

"Ben has them. They went down to the
lake to watch the kayak races."

"By himself?"

"Oh, no—do you really think I'd be this
calm?" Sure, Ben was proving to be the better of the two of them with the kids, but she
wasn't that confident in his abilities. "Leigh
and Logan and their girls are with him."

Victoria looked relieved. "Oh, well, as
long as Leigh is there, they're good." Leigh
was a miracle worker with children. She
could probably handle all six children herself, which made Lindsay question yet again
why her brother and sister-in-law had chosen her for this role.

"Are you all set up on your side?" Victoria asked.

"Almost. Tent is up, scary heart-attack
video cued and ready to cause panic-induced
health kicks for about a week. And the fire-

fighters are here filling the dunk tank. Mark is up first at eight."

She checked her watch. In ten minutes.

"That should be lucrative," Victoria said, her mouth full of coconut.

"We're hoping. Anyway, stay hydrated and out of the sun as much as possible…and make sure to wear sunblock. It's already a scorcher out there and the day hasn't even really started."

"Thanks for the reminder. I will." Victoria dropped into the chair behind the front table and reached for her metal cash box.

"Hey, Mel," Lindsay said before leaving, "why don't you stay here and run Aunt Vic's booth with her?" Last year the little girl had been excited to help her mother and Victoria inside the B and B tent.

Melissa stared at her feet and mumbled, "I'd rather watch the firefighters."

"Really, Lindsay, who wouldn't?" Victoria waved them off. "Go on, sweetheart. Take pictures, okay?"

"Will do, Auntie Vic. I'll post them to Facebook so you can see."

"Facebook? I thought your dad canceled

your page," Lindsay said, knowing she hadn't reactivated it.

Melissa shrugged. "He's not here any-more, is he?"

Victoria's eyes widened.

Lindsay's stomach tightened. "Okay, we'll talk about that later."

At her tent she was relieved to see the dunk tank was full. The ice-cold water would heat in no time with the sun beating down on it. Mark Adams was pulling up in his convertible.

"You're actually on time," she said, check-ing her watch—8:01 a.m.—close enough, anyway. Unlike any date they'd gone on in the past.

"Anything for charity," he said, his charming grin too perfect for so early in the morning.

"Any excuse to show off your body, you mean."

"Hey, this doesn't just happen overnight, you know," he said, flexing his chest mus-cles as he approached the tank, his bleached-blond hair reflecting the sun. He eyed the glass tank. "How cold is the water?"

"Cold," she said.

"Hey, Mark," Melissa said shyly next to her.

He bent and slid his glasses to the top of his head. "Hey, Mel. How are you?"

The girl actually swooned and Lindsay had to take her by the hand. "Come on, I'll give you something to do."

This one was going to be trouble.

"HOW'S IT GOING?" Noah asked Melanie as he watched his buddy and fellow firefighter take a dunk into the tank at noon that day, an hour before his own shift was scheduled to begin.

The park was packed with people enjoying the rides and carnival snacks, and the fund-raising booths were just as busy.

He was happy to see that inside the medical tent no one was being treated for heat stroke yet.

One small boy sat in the Lost and Found, but he didn't seem worried as he ate a Popsicle and colored with Melissa.

"Great! Because of Mark's reputation around town, we've already raised over a thousand dollars. We're thinking about leaving him in there all day," Melanie said with a laugh.

"Forget that." Mark climbed back up onto his perch. "I warmed the water up for you, Noah."

"You better not have peed in there, man," he said.

Melissa giggled. "You're funny."

"Do me a favor and tell your aunt that, okay?"

"Mel, Aunt Vic texted and said they're really busy over at her tent and she could use your help. Can you head over there now, please?" Lindsay asked.

The girl looked ready to protest, but Noah said, "I'll walk you." He tucked his motorcycle helmet under the desk in the tent and took off his leather jacket.

Three females took in his chest and biceps visible through the sweat-drenched shirt clinging to him. Wow, he really must be eye candy if they couldn't take their eyes off someone as sweaty as he was.

As long as Lindsay liked what she saw, he was okay with that.

"She's okay to walk over by herself. It's not far," Lindsay said, earning her a scowl from Melissa.

"Shh, Aunt Lindsay. No I'm not," she told Noah.

Lindsay shook her head as the girl tucked her tiny hand in his.

"I'll be right back," Noah said with a wink.

"I don't understand why Aunt Lindsay doesn't like you," Melissa said as they made their way toward the B and B tent near the kid's splash park and trampoline zone.

Oh, she liked him. He knew that for sure, but he played along. "Me, either, kiddo."

"I mean you're cute and funny…I like boys who are cute and funny."

He frowned. "What boys? You're eight."

"Almost nine. And I've had a boyfriend since kindergarten," she said, tossing her tangled blond ponytail over her shoulder.

He prayed that if he ever had children, he didn't have a girl. "Well, your aunt doesn't approve of my career choice."

"Fighting, right?"

"Yeah."

"It does kind of suck. I mean you'd never hit someone on the street, right?"

"No, of course not…never… I mean unless they were hurting a child or animal or something."

"Naturally," she said with a nod, and he laughed. But his smile faded as she added, "So why is it okay to hit someone in the ring?"

The little girl and her aunt really knew how to make him squirm.

"Well, it's a sport. It's a competition of athletics really. We don't just hit—we kick or submit with choke holds or arm bars…"

That didn't sound much better, he realized.

She wrinkled her nose in disgust as she shook her head. "I think I agree with Aunt Lindsay on this one. Sorry, Noah."

They'd reached the B and B tent and Melissa hurried inside when she saw that the line to buy baked goods extended far past the shade of the canopy.

Well, enlisting the help of the girl to get her aunt's attention was obviously out of the question.

As HIS BODY hit the cool water below him, Noah waved his arms frantically. The water wasn't deep, but it was over his head and the surge to the top took a little longer than he'd expected.

Sputtering, he wiped his eyes as he climbed back onto the perch.

Out of the corner of his eye he saw Lindsay watching him. "Nothing to it," he said through the glass.

She rolled her eyes and returned her attention to the line of people waiting to pay for the opportunity to dunk him. He scanned the long line. He didn't know he'd alienated so many people in Brookhollow.

By the time his first ten-minute break arrived, he'd lost count of how many times he'd hit the water. A lot of people had fantastic aim.

Brookhollow should really consider starting its own baseball team.

Climbing out of the tank, he accepted a towel from Lindsay. "Thank you."

"Thank *you*. So far we've raised another thousand dollars. Keep this up and you'll raise more than Mark."

"I thought people around here liked me better than him," he said, only half teasing. He hadn't dated any of the women in town since moving to Brookhollow from Beach Haven the year before, yet there were far too many women lining up for the opportunity to dunk his butt.

"They do. They like looking at you better, as well," she said before clamping her lips tightly together.

She handed him a bottle of water but he shook his head. "No, thank you, I'm surprised there's any water left in that tank, I've swallowed so much of it." He sat on a bench in the shade of the tent.

"Hey, Noah, great news," Brandon said, walking toward them. "I think we may have another sponsor for your fight next weekend."

"Really?" Excitement rose in his chest. "That's awesome." So far, his only real sponsor was Extreme Athletics and they paid him in free training. The extra payday from sponsors could double his take home from the fight. Right now the money would certainly be appreciated—his bank account was quickly depleting and that month's rent would once again be late. Luckily his coach believed in him enough to know that once he made it to the UFC, money would come.

Next to him, Lindsay's face clouded and she busied herself with the DVD player, restarting the disgusting what-clogged-arteries-look-like video.

His excitement faded. Any mention of fighting around her and she closed off. He stood and moved closer to his coach to continue the conversation away from her.

"Who is it?"

Brandon hesitated. "Um, why don't we meet at the pool hall later and I'll bring the sponsorship clothes they provided."

Clothes? Wow, that was top-of-the-line sponsorship. Usually beginning fighters had to settle for water bottles or towels that would make an appearance on the PPV a couple of times throughout the fight. Clothing sponsors usually held out for the big-name fighters, who would be covered in logos throughout the fight. "Sure… Hey, what are you doing?"

Brandon handed Melanie several bills. "Paying to dunk you."

"Break time's up," Lindsay said, taking the towel from him. "Get back in."

Clearly, she was still annoyed about the sponsorship.

Noah took her by the arm as she moved away. "I tell you what. I'll climb back in there, and you get one shot. If you miss, you go out with me tonight."

"And if you go in, what do I get?"

It was nearly impossible not to kiss her. Wipe that perturbed expression from her face.

"You get to go out with me tonight," he said, trying to pull her toward his still-wet body.

She resisted with a laugh. "Nice try. How about, if you go in, you help me take all of this stuff back to the clinic later today."

He nodded. "Okay, deal." The way he saw it, either way he'd get a chance to spend time with her.

She waited for him to climb back into the tank. Before he'd barely gotten comfortable she took aim and his butt hit the water.

Dammit.

He wiped his face as he came to the surface. She stood smiling at him.

"I have to catch up with Ben and the kids. I'll be back at five to start packing up," she said with a wink.

He watched as she skipped off toward the fairgrounds.

Climbing back onto the seat for the millionth time, he sighed when he saw his coach was next.

"Don't get too comfy," Brandon said, releasing the ball.

"HEY, GUYS. HOW are the fairgrounds?" Lindsay asked. Ben was pushing the twin's double stroller; the boys, shooting each other with water guns, in tow. She'd been relieved when they'd been excited about going that morning and it eased her stress a little to see them laughing and having fun.

"Great," he said, but he sounded exhausted. Three hours alone at the fair with four children would be a challenge for anyone. "The kids were getting hungry, so we were heading toward the food carts. Do you have time to eat?"

"Yeah," she said, taking Jacob and Caleb's hands as they made their way to the concession stands. "Are you guys having fun?"

Jacob nodded, leaning around her to shoot a stream of water at his brother. "Ben bought us these awesome water guns."

"Bought them? I thought you had to win them at the games?"

"Usually you do," Caleb said. "But the man behind the booth said Ben had spent so much money trying to win them he could have bought eight, so he gave us two."

"Thanks, guys," Ben said.

"Not such a great aim?" Lindsay asked, trying not to laugh.

"Well, those hit-the-target games aren't really designed to win anyway," he said defensively.

"I bet Aunt Lindsay could do it," Noah said from behind them.

She turned. "What are you doing out of the dunk tank?"

He smiled. "Fate must have been smiling on me...Brandon broke the lever."

"What? Seriously?" Brandon and his stupid big muscles.

"Afraid so."

"That's fantastic," she grumbled. Losing the dunk tank profits halfway through the afternoon wasn't ideal.

"Don't worry. Brandon and Extreme Athletics offered to pay to fix it and they donated a thousand dollars to the clinic to make up for any funds lost."

She sighed and eased the tension out of her shoulders. "Where is he? I should go thank him. Even with you in there we'd never have raised that much this afternoon."

"He left. But we're meeting tonight at the pool hall if you want to join us."

She glanced at Ben who was watching the boys chase each other around the babies' stroller. She knew he was listening and waiting to hear her answer.

"I can't tonight. I'll send him a thank-you card from the clinic. But when you see him, let him know I appreciate the donation."

"Will do." Noah glanced between her and Ben and the kids, and the silence grew awkward until he finally said, "Well, I'll see you at the booth at five to help take it down."

"WHERE SHOULD I put this stuff?" Noah asked as they struggled to carry their armloads in through the back door of the clinic.

Lindsay hesitated. How on earth had all of this stuff been packed in here the day before? It seemed impossible the tent and all of the exhibit stuff had been stored in this tiny room. "Um…"

"Don't rush. It's not heavy," Noah said, groaning behind her.

She turned, her hands on her hips. "I thought you were supposed to be strong or something?"

"My muscles are still frozen from that 30-degree water you insisted on dunking me in, remember?"

How could she forget? Noah's shirtless body on the dunk-tank platform had made it impossible to focus on running the health-clinic booth. Luckily there hadn't been any heat-stroke patients.

"Sorry, let me quickly move a few things…" She put her own load down then rearranged several boxes on the storage shelves, before turning to take one of the boxes from him.

Her arms dipped and she struggled to catch the thirty-pound box before it slipped out of her hands. And he was carrying three of these? She set it aside and reached for another one.

He shook his head. "Move aside. I'll stack them."

She moved past him back out into the hall. When he came out to join her, she closed the door and locked it.

"Wow, thank you. I didn't realize the clinic had accumulated so much over the years."

"Yeah, no problem," he said, wiping his forehead with the back of his arm.

"You thirsty?" She was and she hadn't done much of the work.

"A soda would be great if you have one."

"Follow me." She led the way through the clinic to the staff lunchroom, pausing at the door. "Technically, you're not allowed in here, but I'll make an exception for today."

She flicked on the light and went to the fridge. "All I have is diet."

"I'll take it. I still need to cut three pounds before my weigh-ins anyway." He leaned against the counter.

"Here you are," she said, handing him a soda and opening one for herself.

Lindsay watched as he guzzled the soda and tossed the can into the blue recycle bin near the door.

She took a sip of hers, fighting the urge to bring up the subject of the sponsorship. But the prolonged silence only served to make her acutely aware that they were alone. "So, who is your new sponsor?"

"Brandon said he'd tell me about it later tonight. It really doesn't matter—any sponsor is better than none." He paused, studying her. "Look, I know you'd rather not talk about this stuff, so let's not..." He lowered his gaze on her lips.

"What?" she asked, playing with the rim of the can.

"I'm trying to remember what your lips feel like."

Talking about the sponsorship seemed like a better discussion. It was one that reminded her why she'd yet to kiss him again.

One that reminded her that despite all of the things she liked about Noah, there was one deal breaker that they couldn't move past.

He took a step toward her and she took a step back.

"You're not even supposed to be in here..."

Noah reached for her and pulled her closer. Taking her soda from her, he took a sip and set the can on the counter behind him. "I won't tell anyone if you don't," he murmured against her ear.

A shiver danced down her spine and her entire body came alive. "Noah...I don't know what you think you're doing..."

"I'm going to kiss you again. Isn't it obvious from the way I'm whispering against your ear...?" he whispered. "The way I'm tightening my grip on your hips to keep you in my arms..." His grip tightened. "And the way I'm lowering my head toward yours..."

Lindsay swallowed hard when his gaze locked with hers, his lips an inch above hers. She closed her eyes slowly, waiting in anticipation of a kiss she didn't want to fight. Blame it on weeks of turmoil and life-changing events or the way he smelled faintly of the promise of summer—it didn't matter. She wanted this kiss…from him… right now.

So where was it?

She opened her eyes and frowned as she saw him still standing there, staring at her, his lips a fraction of an inch away but still not touching hers.

"Noah. Are you going to kiss me or not?"

"Why don't you help me out here, Lindsay? I've come as far as I go, the rest is up to you," he said hoarsely as his eyes flitted between hers and her mouth.

She didn't hesitate, stepping closer into his embrace and reaching up to wrap her arms around his neck as her lips met his.

Noah's hands left her hips and circled her neck, his fingers tangling in her hair as he deepened the kiss.

If common sense was voicing its concern, Lindsay certainly wasn't paying attention as her hands slid down his arms and she appreciated the strength in his biceps, resting her hands on his at her neck.

He broke away then, and when his eyes opened, the affection she saw there took her breath away more than the kiss had. He brushed his hand along her cheek. "I was lying."

She blinked. "Huh?" Lying? About what? At that moment she could barely remember her own name let alone any discussion they may have had in the past ten minutes.

"When I said I was trying to remember what your lips felt like." He touched her bottom lip with his thumb. "I remembered— too well."

"Was it as good the second time?"

He pretended to think, wrapping his arms around her once more. "Hard to know for sure… I think I need to try it again…"

CHAPTER TEN

AFTER A QUICK shower and a protein shake, Noah hopped on his motorcycle and headed to the pool hall to meet Brandon.

When he walked in, several guys from the MMA club and some of his coworkers at the fire hall were standing around a corner table laughing loudly at something Brandon had said. They sobered quickly when they saw him.

Something was up. "Hey, guys, what's so funny?"

"It's actually not funny…in fact…it's really quite serious," Ethan said, tapping him on the shoulder before bursting into another fit of laughter.

"Yeah, I don't think it's something to joke about," Ethan's brother, Jim, said, turning his head to smother a laugh of his own.

"Someone care to enlighten me about the joke I'm obviously the butt of?" Noah asked, sitting across from Brandon. What were all of these guys doing here anyway?

Brandon reached into a bag next to him, pulled out a bright yellow piece of fabric and tossed it to him.

Noah read the hot-pink logo on the thin, stretchy fabric and stared in disbelief. This had to be a joke. He turned the shorts around in his hand. "Tinactin?"

Brandon tried desperately to look serious. "Your new sponsor I was telling you about. Congrats."

The men started laughing again and Noah shook his head. "An athlete's-foot cream?"

"Look, you're a new fighter. Everlast isn't exactly knocking on your door. And what's wrong with these shorts?" Brandon said before choking on another laugh.

Noah tossed the briefs to his coach.

"Forget it, Brandon. I refuse to embarrass myself in front of millions of viewers."

"Win or lose the fight, they'll give you five grand."

His mouth gaped. "Five grand?"

The temptation was too strong. He needed

the cash. "Let me see the…shorts…again," he said, taking them from his manager.

He held them up and stretched the fabric.

Next to him, Luke Dawson took the shorts and tossed them back to Brandon. "Tell the kid the truth," he said.

Noah glanced between the two men. What was Luke talking about?

Brandon grinned. "We were messing with you." He nodded toward Luke. "Luke's company—Dawson's Architecture—is your new sponsor."

Relieved, he turned to Luke. "Wow, thanks, man." Then he paused. "Please tell me you're not expecting me to wear shorts like those."

Luke laughed, handing him a pair of black boxer briefs instead. The Dawson's Architecture logo was across the back.

These he could handle.

Around him, the other men were still laughing.

"I can't believe you were actually considering wearing these," Brandon said.

His coach had no idea.

THREE MISSED CALLS. Lindsay smiled as she took her phone out of her purse in the clinic's lunchroom a week later. Normally if a guy called her that much, she'd consider changing her number and listing his profile on Stalker.com, but since it was Noah, she decided his persistence was cute.

But a second glance at the numbers revealed only one call was actually from Noah. One was from her mother—of course—and the other was from Henderson Law Firm, her brother's lawyer's office. She frowned. They hadn't left a voice mail. It had been weeks since the accident; what could they possibly need to speak to her about now?

Rebecca popped her head around the corner of the lunchroom door. "Hey, Lindsay, you have a visitor."

The way she said it, Lindsay knew exactly who it was. Dropping her phone into her purse, she made her way down the hall, pulling her hair out of the ponytail as she went.

"Hey, pretty girl," Noah said.

"I don't answer a call and you stalk me?" she said, pulling him through the clinic door to talk outside...so she could hug him without onlookers.

"Not that I wouldn't stalk you, but I actually stopped by to give you these," he said, handing her two tickets for the MMA fight in Newark.

Her excitement over seeing him faded. "I told you I didn't think I could come."

He lifted her chin and placed a kiss on her nose. "I know you did, and I'm not forcing you to. Every fight they give me extra tickets—for family, I guess—and I usually toss them, but I thought maybe…" He shrugged.

Way to pull on the heartstrings, Noah. "Playing the 'my mom walked out and my dad's useless card' is not playing fair, you know."

He laughed and hugged her to his chest. He'd always been rock-hard solid, but the past few days leading up to the fight weigh-ins, he was even more rock-cut and stronger.

"You don't have to come. Sell them on eBay if you want. I thought I'd give them to you in case by some miracle you had the urge to watch—"

"You knock some poor helpless guy on his butt?" she said, finishing his sentence. "Doesn't seem likely."

He kissed her forehead before releasing her. "Okay, but I had to try."

She cleared her throat, flicking the tickets against her fingers. "When do you leave for Newark?"

"Tomorrow morning. So, the other reason I stopped by...I was hoping you'd let me watch you eat tonight."

She frowned. "That doesn't sound stalkerish at all."

"I still have half a pound to cut, so Brandon has me on a liquid diet this week until after the weigh-ins, but I'd like to take you out."

"I'd love to tease you with a juicy steak you can't eat, but Ben's in Newark today, so after work I'm picking the kids up from summer camp and Leigh's, and we're planning to have a picnic. I'd invite you...but I really need some time one-on-one with them."

He nodded. "I understand."

She sensed he didn't, but Ben would be heading back to Newark soon and she had to talk to the kids about how the six of them could make things work without him.

Also, there was something she'd promised Jacob they would do.

"I'll call you later?" She handed him the tickets.

"Keep them in case you have a change of heart." He kissed her quickly on the forehead and headed to his motorcycle.

"Hey, Noah! Break a leg?"

He shook his head as he put on his helmet. "You don't say that when there's an actual possibility I could, crazy girl."

He blew her a kiss and started the bike.

LINDSAY SET THE picnic basket down on the tall, overgrown grass of the B and B yard later that evening. Unfolding her red-and-white-checked blanket, she tossed it into the air. "Mel, can you grab the other side?" she asked, lowering it to the ground, where Jacob and Caleb immediately sat on the edges to keep it from folding in the wind.

She took Mackenzie and Abigail out of the stroller and set them next to their brothers before opening the picnic basket. She'd gone to Joey's diner on the way home to pick up sandwiches, salad and dessert.

Then she'd stopped at the home-and-garden store and bought two small maple trees.

The little boys sat with their tiny plastic shovels clutched in their hands.

"Should we eat or plant first?" she asked.

"Plant!" they both said.

"Melissa, you okay with that?"

The girl nodded, standing and picking up one of the trees. "Where did you guys decide you want to plant them?" she asked her brothers.

"Over by Elmer," Jacob said.

"Can you two manage the other tree?" Lindsay asked, taking Abigail and Mackenzie's hands to lead them across the yard toward where the family's pet guinea pig was buried.

They gathered around the tiny seedling that had been Elmer's memorial, and Lindsay, using the larger shovel she'd brought, dug two holes, making sure they were far enough apart to grow.

A few minutes later when both trees had been planted, they all stood back to admire their work. She didn't profess to have a green thumb and they weren't perfect, but they would be a beautiful reminder of the children's parents.

"Good job, guys," Lindsay told them, wrapping an arm around each of the boys.

"Yeah, it's really cool," Mel agreed. "I miss them so much."

The boys' expressions saddened. "Me, too," Jacob said.

"Me, three," Caleb added.

"Me, four," Lindsay said, hugging them tighter and offering Melissa a reassuring smile.

Caleb glanced at Abby and Mackenzie. "Do you think they miss Mom and Dad?"

Lindsay swallowed a lump in her throat as she watched the baby girls run around the yard. "Yeah, I think they do."

She sat on the grass and motioned for the kids to sit.

Keep it together. Just get through what you need to say.

"I know the past six weeks have been tough and…I'll never be able to replace your parents…but I'm going to try my best to make sure you kids are always loved, always safe and always have someone you can depend on. I'm going to make mistakes and I'm not always going to do things the way your parents would have, but I love all of you so much…"

Great, so much for keeping it together, she thought as her eyes filled with tears.

She gathered them all in for a group hug, knowing this was one challenge in her life she couldn't run away from. And she no longer wanted to.

Jacob kissed her cheek, wiping away a tear with his tiny hand. "Don't worry, Aunt Lindsay. We're a team. We will take care of you, too."

CHAPTER ELEVEN

THE PREFIGHT SESSIONS and weigh-ins Friday evening were a zoo of sports reporters, fans, fighters and their families, and coaches rushing from one scheduled media event to another at the Newark Marriott Conference Center. The big-name fighters were bombarded with requests for autographs as they made their way through the crowds and the lesser-known guys blended into the sea of people, starving and praying they made the weight cut.

When Noah had weighed himself that morning he'd been half a pound under the maximum requirement for the light heavyweight bout. By the next day he'd be ten pounds over, that's how it worked, but for now, his stomach rumbled and he was desperate to weigh in and get back to his hotel.

He was looking forward to a quick final workout followed by a great meal then the hot tub and sauna while he attempted to quiet his mind and prepare mentally for the fight ahead of him.

Following Brandon down the hall to the Grand Ballroom where the weigh-ins had already started, he took several deep breaths. Squaring off with his opponent for the pre-fight photos didn't faze him. Mentally he was tough; a stare-down couldn't shake him.

It was that scale that had him on edge.

"You're sure that scale at the gym was calibrated properly, right?" he asked Brandon as they flashed their access passes to the security guards at the door.

"I guess we're about to find out," his coach said as they entered the standing-room-only space and headed toward the fighters' section.

Calvin Sparks, the owner of TKO Fighting, was at the podium, announcing the weight of a lightweight contender Noah recognized from his last match. The kid might weigh a hundred and forty-five pounds, but a hundred and thirty of it was muscle.

His taller, less muscular opponent stood, looking slightly nervous, waiting to square off. The rest of the fighters gathered on opposite sides of the stage in the conference room.

Opponents, whether the prefight hype had been a personal battle or not, were supposed to stand on opposite sides from each other. But Noah didn't see Romeo Rodriguez, the guy he was scheduled to fight tomorrow night.

"Brandon, do you see Rodriguez over there?" he whispered.

Brandon shook his head.

As the weigh-ins continued, Noah began to grow nervous. Where was the guy? The fighters weighed in one by one and squared off with their opponent for the media shot, then went their separate ways. When his turn came, he fought to keep his hands steady as he stepped onto the scale.

One eighty-six.

A pound over.

They'd allow that.

Stepping down, Noah waited to see Rodriguez appear.

Instead a guy he didn't recognize took the stage. A big man. There's no way he would be fighting him—the guy would never come in under one eighty-five.

Locating Brandon at the back of the room, he frowned.

Brandon shrugged, his eyes wide.

"Next up, we have light heavyweight fighter Craig Selers. He will be replacing Romeo Rodriguez in the fight against Noah Parks.

"Rodriguez suffered a torn hamstring in training yesterday," Calvin told the reporters.

Noah, his eyes glued to his new opponent, barely heard him.

When Selers took the scale, Noah held his breath. He wasn't sure if fighting an unknown beast was better or worse than having the fight canceled. He needed the money from this fight, but he also valued his life. He'd never even heard of this guy before, so he had no idea of his fighting style or record.

"One eighty-six. He's good," the official at the scale told Calvin, sounding slightly surprised himself.

Seriously? The guy must have chicken legs to pull off that weight with an extreme upper body that made Noah look like a teenage boy.

He squared off with his new opponent and cringed when the guy didn't even raise his hands. Clearly he didn't believe in sportsmanship, which usually meant he would be a brawler in the cage.

Unfortunately, Noah had trained to defend against a jujitsu fighter. A ground game he'd prepared for. Fifteen minutes ducking punches hadn't been part of his strategy for winning this fight.

A moment later he and Brandon left the conference. "Well, this is not ideal," Brandon said.

Noah fired a look at his coach. "You think? There's no way that guy should have made weight."

"His head must be hollow," Brandon grumbled, punching the button on the elevator.

"Great. My shots won't affect him."

"Look, let's not start to panic yet. You're a great fighter. We'll go online to research the guy's previous fights tonight and work on a new game plan."

So much for the hot tub and sauna. Calming his mind? He'd be lucky if he got any sleep.

Another fighter—a flyweight about half Noah's size—joined them in the elevator. He looked sympathetically at Noah. "It's days like this I'm glad to be in the flyweight division."

"Why's that?" Noah asked, though he'd give up his six-foot, muscular frame for the kid's athletic, lanky build to get out of this fight.

"Selers is a killer. He put his opponent in the hospital after each of his last three fights." The elevator doors opened and the kid got out. "Good luck."

Noah looked at Brandon. "Can we panic a little now?"

THE CLINIC WAS SLOW, which only served to give Lindsay time to think about what she wasn't doing tonight.

Noah had texted her to say everything had gone well at the weigh-ins and he would see her on Sunday evening. She'd wished him good luck, even though she wasn't sure she'd meant it entirely, and had been worried sick and confused ever since. Sure, he'd fought before. Heck, she'd treated his injuries, but this time was different.

This time it wasn't gorgeous Noah Parks, a guy she'd never consider dating, who was fighting.

This time it was Noah Parks, a man she was undoubtedly falling in love with, who was fighting.

She groaned. This was going to be the longest day ever. Waiting to hear from him, waiting to hear the fight went well, was going to be torture.

You could go and see for yourself.

She'd told him not to expect her there, and he'd accepted that. She wouldn't change her mind. Besides, it was too late and she had to work.

A quick glance toward the waiting room revealed what it had all day long: empty. She sighed. At least if she was seeing patients and keeping busy, the time would pass quickly and she'd have less time to second guess her decision.

As she filed the patient folders that had collected on top of the file cabinet during their busy week, she pulled his. All three MRIs were fine.

She scanned his treatment list for the past year; a sprained wrist and four stitches above his right eye seemed to be the only real injuries he'd suffered after his fights, other than bruising of the ribs, which had been so severe she'd been shocked when the X-rays revealed no broken bones. Sighing again, she put the folder away. There was only one way to know if she could handle being in a relationship with an MMA fighter.

Closing the file cabinet, she headed to the staff lunchroom where Rebecca was texting on her phone. "Hey, Rebecca?"

"Oh, sorry… Is it getting busy out there?" The girl stashed her phone quickly.

"Not at all. I'm actually contemplating examining myself at this point. Um, do you think you can handle the close on your own?"

Lindsay checked her watch. It was five o'clock. The clinic closed at nine. The emergency staff nurses were even more bored upstairs and Rebecca could call one of them down to the clinic if half of Brookhollow suddenly got sick in the next four hours.

"Of course. You okay?"

Other than losing her mind?

"I'm good. I think I'll head out early."

"Okay. See you tomorrow," Rebecca said, gathering a stack of magazines to read at the front desk.

In the parking lot a few minutes later Lindsay turned the key in the ignition of the minivan. The engine sputtered and roared, then died. "What the…?" She tried again. "Come on." Nothing.

Seriously? This was happening now? Maybe it was a sign she shouldn't go. Leaning her head back against her seat, she whispered a silent, desperate prayer and tried the key again. This time the engine wouldn't even offer a false promise of a purr.

Stupid Doug Cooper had sold her a lemon.

She dialed the number to Bailey's Place, then opened the door and tossed her legs outside as the phone at the garage continued to ring. "Come on, Bailey…"

"Bailey's Place," Bailey, out of breath, huffed a second later.

"Bailey, thank God. I was afraid Nick was working." Bailey's cousin was an amazing detail expert but he still had a lot to learn about actually fixing vehicles. "It's Lindsay. My minivan," she said through clenched teeth, "won't start."

"The one you just bought?"

Would she ever own more than one? "That would be the one, yes."

"What's the problem?"

"Seriously, Bailey?" How was she supposed to know? She was a nurse. People she could fix—or at least try to. Vehicles were not her area of expertise.

"Right, sorry. Give me ten minutes. I'm just finishing up with a customer and then I'll be on my way with the tow truck."

Eleven minutes later the tow truck pulled into the clinic parking lot and Bailey, dressed in her dark blue coveralls, her long dark hair in a ponytail, jumped down. "Pop the hood for me."

Lindsay climbed out. "Wouldn't even know how," she said.

Bailey laughed. "In addition to my self-defense classes, I think I need to start teaching Basic Vehicle Maintenance for Women."

"Unless you held the class in the parking lot of Extreme Athletics, your turnout probably wouldn't be as great."

"Unfortunately, I think you're right," she said, popping the hood. She disappeared beneath it and Lindsay fanned herself with the fight tickets as she waited in the afternoon heat.

Maybe if she asked Lily to come along, she could drive if the van refused to start. She bit her lip. Her friend had already said no, and she understood her hesitancy to return to Newark where her ex-husband was serving time for domestic abuse.

"Your radiator looks to be the problem. Maybe overheated. I'll have to tow it to the shop and have a look."

Great. "How long do you think it will take?" If Rachel had been here, she'd have convinced her sister-in-law to tag along... and she could've driven them. Lindsay missed her.

"A day or two. I'll bump it ahead. I still

owe you for that petition you started for the insurance claim on the garage last year."

Right. When Bailey's shop had burned down. The woman didn't owe her anything, but who was she to argue now? "Okay, thanks, Bailey." A day or two was better than a few weeks.

Bailey closed the hood and came toward her. "What are those?" she asked, eyeing the tickets in Lindsay's hand.

"Tickets to the MMA fights in Newark tonight. Noah gave them to me."

Maybe the van breaking down had been the wake-up she'd needed to regain her senses.

"You were going to go?" Bailey asked in surprise.

"I was thinking about it for, like, three seconds." Lindsay shrugged.

"Can't your plus-one drive?"

"I asked Lily to come with me but she'd already said no…and I don't feel like forcing the issue with her for obvious reasons." She went to tuck the tickets away, but Bailey grabbed them.

"These are cage-side seats." Her eyes were wide.

"Yeah." As if being closer to the action was a good thing. She shuddered at the thought.

"No, Lindsay. Like, cage side. Like, you can smell the sweat and blood from these seats."

"Gross." Bailey was definitely one of the guys if she thought that was a selling feature.

"Jump in the truck, we're going to these fights. I'll drive." She smiled ear-to-ear as she reached for her cell. "Ethan's going to be so jealous."

TWO HOURS LATER the women entered the arena in Newark, showing their front-of-the-line VIP passes to the guy at the door. The look he gave them spoke volumes as he took in her nurse's uniform and Bailey's coveralls.

"We look ridiculous," Lindsay said as they joined the crowd inside. The sign out front had said the event was sold out. The sport had a huge following and, with the fights not yet sanctioned in New York City, the fans flocked to Newark for their MMA entertainment. "Are you at least wearing something underneath those?" She gestured at Bailey's coveralls.

"In this heat—no." Bailey scanned the busy entrance. "Over there—merchandise tables." She pointed to the right where several tables were covered with MMA paraphernalia.

"Well, I guess anything is better than this," Lindsay said, but she was rethinking the statement a moment later when she stared at her options. "Who are these T-shirts made for?" she asked, holding up a size-large tank top touting As Real As It Gets. It looked like it might fit Melissa.

Or a previous version of herself might have squeezed into it, she abruptly realized.

"They stretch," Bailey said, grabbing a man's shirt and a pair of shorts.

Lindsay took the tank top and searched for something other than the very-short shorts that part of her still thought were incredibly cute…but not appropriate for a thirty-five-year-old stepmother of five, she reminded herself.

"I'll just wear these pants. Kids are wearing them to be cool these days, right?"

Bailey wasn't listening. She was chatting with two fighters behind the merchandise table as she paid for her clothing.

She was completely star-struck, Lindsay thought, watching the interaction. At least someone would enjoy the evening's events.

"Hey, Linds, can you take a pic?" Bailey asked, pulling her closer and handing her a cell phone.

"Sure." Lindsay set her clothes aside and took the picture of Bailey squeezed between the two tall, muscular guys in MMA T-shirts.

"Thank you," Bailey told them as Lindsay paid for her things.

"Are you going to show that picture to Ethan?"

Bailey laughed. "Texting it to him right now," she said as they headed toward the washrooms to change.

Ten minutes later, while Bailey took their clothes out to the truck, Lindsay texted

Brandon to say they were headed for their seats.

As she walked through the crowded arena, her nerves danced. The excitement and adrenaline coming off the fans was invigorating but at the same time made her stomach lurch.

These fights were no joke. Could she really watch Noah get hit? Could she really watch him hit someone else? She'd seen him train, but that was different. She knew once he stepped inside the ring, she would see a different side of the man she was falling in love with. One she wasn't sure she was going to like.

Lindsay searched for Brandon in the back of the arena near the dressing rooms. She didn't want to distract Noah, but now that she was there, all she wanted was to see him.

"Lindsay!" Brandon's voice cut through the noise in the hallway. "You made it."

"I haven't sat through the fights yet, but so far, so good," she said, relieved to see a familiar face. "How is he?"

"Oh, just great," Brandon said, but he was frowning.

"What's wrong?"

"Nothing."

"Tell me or I'm leaving." She needed little coaxing to leave the stadium and head back to Brookhollow. If she could force Bailey away from the fight to drive her back, that is.

Brandon sighed. "The guy Noah was supposed to fight got injured last minute in training, so he's facing a different opponent. One we hadn't prepared for."

Her stomach did a flip-flop. Fantastic. She was going to see him get crushed .

"Are they allowed to do that? Hardly seems fair."

"Lindsay, this is MMA, not tennis. The rules are…flexible. Anyway, we got this. I'm not worried," Brandon said, shrugging.

She wasn't buying it. "Oh, really? Well, why do you look like you're about to pee in your pants?"

He pulled her aside and lowered his voice. "Because I'm freaking out," he admitted. "This dude is big. And he's only had three fights—all knockouts. We watched YouTube videos last night…" He paused.

It felt as if all the blood had drained out of her body. "I knew coming here was a bad idea. I should leave." Watching Noah get knocked out… She couldn't do it.

"No!" Brandon grabbed her arm as she turned to look for the nearest exit. "You have to stay. Come talk to him. I've never seen him so worried before a fight. His confidence is shaken, but if he sees that you're here, that you support him in this…"

"I didn't say I support him in this."

"For his sake tonight, pretend you do."

NOAH TRIED TO focus his energy on hitting his targets in front of him and not on the panic creeping into his chest. The kid in the elevator had been right. Selers was a killer. And, after watching the man's fights the night before, he felt sick. Not better, as he had hoped.

Everyone had holes in their game, a predictably timed punch or a repetitive fighting style that could be counted on to develop a counterattack. Not Selers. His fighting style was unpredictable, inconsistent and he seemed to like punching things—a lot and hard. Noah suspected they would remain on their feet without a lot of ground game. His hope for a submission win while he was still conscious was quickly fading, along with his confidence.

He'd been so sure of a win with this fight. He needed this seventh straight win to secure his spot on the UFC fight card in August. His career depended on it.

Somehow he had to find a way to dig deep and leave it all in the cage. Everything he had.

The door behind him opened and his assistant trainer, Dex, lowered the punch shields as he nodded behind him.

Noah wiped his forehead and turned. A smile teased his lips. "You made it."

"So far..." Lindsay said, scanning the locker room. She kept her back close to the wall and he noticed the discomfort on her face.

But she was here.

"So, this is where you practice?" she asked, avoiding his eyes.

She was nervous and it was cute. It almost eased his own fear and anxiety. "This is where I warm up and train, yeah," he said, moving toward her and her obviously new, dark blue MMA tank top. "You bought a merchandise shirt?"

"When in Rome, right?"

Glancing down, he noticed the pants from her nurse's uniform. She'd come straight from work. Obviously this had been a last-minute decision.

"Bailey's here, too," she said.

"Let me guess. She's in the autograph line."

"Not yet, but I'm sure once she discovers that table, she will be."

She was really uncomfortable. He wrapped his arms around her and buried his face in her hair, breathing in the soft scent of jasmine.

"Thank you for coming, but you really don't have to watch the fights." He took comfort in knowing she was here, but she had yet to smile. He didn't like her doing something she wasn't comfortable with, especially now since her worst fears over the brutality were more than likely about to be confirmed.

She shook her head. "I'm here. Don't worry, I won't bail now."

He might.

"Okay. Well, stay with Brandon."

"Shouldn't I stay in my assigned seat?" She held out her ticket.

"Once the fights start, yeah. But in the meantime, I worry about you in this crowd by yourself. The fans can get a little rowdy. And once the fight starts, you can cover your eyes or chat with the ring girls," he said with a laugh.

She nodded.

"Ready?" Brandon asked, entering.

Nope. "Let's do it."

Leaning forward Noah pressed a quick kiss to Lindsay's lips. "Will you put me back together once the fight is over?" he whispered, moving her blond curls away from her face with his wrapped hands and sparring gloves, letting them rest on her shoulders while his gaze searched hers.

Her smile was small, but it was there. "I always do."

That's all he needed.

CLIMBING INSIDE THE cage had never bothered him before, but that evening Noah had to admit, the temptation to run in the opposite direction was strong.

Bouncing from one foot to the other, he heard the octagon door click shut and his heart beat in his chest.

He forced several deep breaths as he stared across the mat at his opponent. Their eyes met and he refused to look away, as the referee called them in.

"We want a clean fair fight. You've gone over the rules with your corner. You ready?" he asked Selers.

The beast nodded.

"You ready?" he asked him.

He must have nodded as well, because a second later the ref yelled, "Fight!"

Pure adrenaline coursed through him as they circled one another, both weighing their opponent's game plan. Then a second later, Selers went in for the take-down.

Somehow above the noise of the crowd, he heard Brandon's voice and he sprawled to defend against being tossed to the mat. A sure and painful defeat was awaiting him there.

Selers moved away, and landed several jabs. Noah blinked.

The guy's hands were like bricks contacting with his chin.

He retreated slightly and caught sight of Lindsay's terrified expression as she watched, one hand half covering her face.

His only thought was that he couldn't put her through much more of this.

HIS KNOCK-OUT KICK came from a place no one, including himself, would have expected. The crowd cheered wildly around him as he spun in direct contrast to the undeniable snapping sound of his leg, followed by the searing pain firing his right leg.

But he was alive. And he'd won the fight. And right now the adrenaline rushing through him after eleven minutes of the toughest fight of his career made it impossible to worry about the pain.

As his body hit the mat and the referee officially called the fight, Brandon and the medic were at Noah's side.

"I can't believe you won," Brandon said.

"Thanks for the confidence, coach," he

said, wincing as the medic adjusted the leg. It hurt, but the adrenaline pumping through him dulled the pain...for now.

He scanned the cage-side crowd for Lindsay. Bailey was waving excitedly at him; there was no sign of Lindsay. "Where is she?"

"She ran to the bathroom the minute your leg bent in that disgusting way."

Crap. "Sounds about right," he said, blinking to remain conscious as a sudden wave of heat followed immediately by a chill ran through him. "I'm feeling kind of nauseous myself," he added as they lifted him onto the red medic stretcher. "Wait. How's Selers?"

He turned his head to see his opponent still out on the mat, the doctor hovering above him, along with the fighter's coach and trainers.

"He okay?" He'd been out for more than a few seconds, which was never good. Guilt washed over Noah as it always did whenever he injured an opponent.

"He's waking up," Brandon reassured him, placing a hand on his chest to prevent him from sitting up as they lifted the stretcher.

"Going to have one heck of a headache, though. By the way, where did that kick come from? I never knew your leg could go so high."

"Me, either. Don't expect to see it again," Noah mumbled as his eyes closed.

LINDSAY ENTERED THE medical room where Noah was having a cast applied to his right leg.

"Hi," she said as she joined him next to the bed.

"Feel better?" he asked with a loopy grin and slightly slurred speech. No doubt he'd been given a lot of painkillers while they'd reset the fractured bone.

"I should be asking you that," she said, standing to the side as the medic finished applying the cast.

"I'm great. I feel fantastic."

"That's what the drugs are for," she said, glancing at his leg. She'd heard the snap from her cage-side seat before she'd seen the leg twist as both men hit the mat.

Seeing him fight was even worse than she'd ever imagined.

"Hey, pretty girl, you okay?" he asked, lifting her chin to look at her.

He seemed quite lucid now in his concern over her.

"I'm fine," she said, but it was far from the truth. She wasn't fine.

"It really wasn't as bad as it looked."

"That's good news, because it was the worst thing I've ever seen."

"You're a nurse. You see injuries all the time." He reached for her hand as the medic moved away, signing his treatment and release form.

"I see the aftermath of the injuries. I don't usually see them happen." She shuddered.

"I won and I'm okay. The doctor thinks it's just a hairline fracture, he set the cast just to be safe." He paused. "And I'm sure Selers will be fine. Brandon said he was waking up as they carried me out." He tucked her hand close to his body and rested his head back against the bed.

"That doesn't mean he's going to be fine. That kick could have killed him." She looked away, trying but failing to see the sweet, caring Noah she'd started to fall in love with.

But all she could see was the blow to his opponent's head that had knocked the man out cold.

"Lindsay, we're fighters. We train for this," he said as his eyelids fluttered shut. "Looks like I'll get that fight in August now," he mumbled, his head falling slightly to the side as he released her hand.

She frowned as she shook him awake. "August?" He couldn't be serious. "No way—your leg is going to take months to heal…and then there's the rehab…"

His goofy smile was proof the painkillers had really kicked in now. "Don't worry, I heal fast. And with you as my nurse, I'll be good as new in no time." He reached for her hand again.

She pulled it away. The man was crazy if he thought he'd be ready to fight again in a month. He was crazy to even want to. And if he thought she was going to nurse him back to health so he could do more damage to himself or yet another fighter, he was sadly mistaken. She refused to keep piecing him back together, just so he could rip himself apart again.

Even though she'd promised to.

"Hey, come back," he said, wiggling closer to the edge of the bed to reach for her again.

She folded her arms across her chest. "Don't," she said.

"Lindsay...I'm fine."

"This time. Personally, I think you got lucky with that kick. That guy should have crushed you."

"Wow, that hurts more than the leg."

She studied her shaky hands in front of her and cleared her throat, eyeing the cast on his propped-up leg. "I thought I could do it, Noah... I was wrong." She shrugged. "Watching you get hurt tonight...even just seeing you step inside that cage with that monster-size man..."

"Lindsay, come here, please."

She couldn't. She couldn't continue this with him. He couldn't say she hadn't tried. She had.

She leaned forward and kissed his cheek, letting her lips linger a second longer than was safe. "There's no way I can keep watching you get hurt."

She squeezed his hand then, turning, left the room.

IT WAS AFTER midnight when Lindsay quietly turned the key in her door and cringed as it creaked opened. She turned and waved to Bailey, who was backing the tow truck out the driveway.

The living-room television was the only sign of life in the dark house, flashes of light from the screen escaping out into the hall and reflecting off the walls.

Shoot, Ben must be waiting up for her. Suddenly she felt like a teenager sneaking in past curfew, desperate to avoid parents waiting for an explanation.

She removed her shoes, a habit from childhood, and put them in the closet next to the children's shoes lined up neatly from biggest to smallest. Then, taking a deep breath, she walked toward the living room.

It was only Ben. And just because they were currently both living in her house and raising these kids together didn't mean she owed him any explanation about where she'd been or who she'd been with. They weren't a couple.

An image of Noah flashed in her mind as she reached the entryway to the living room. They weren't a couple, either. Not anymore.

Seeing him fight had reinforced everything she'd believed about the sport. He'd won. But from where she was sitting, she hadn't seen a winner in that fight. Just one broken bone and a concussion. It didn't matter that Noah's arm had been raised in victory.

And now, he'd lost her. She couldn't help but wonder if that mattered to him. Obviously not enough.

Rounding the corner, she stopped short.

Ben lay on the couch with Abby and Mackenzie curled up next to him. Abby slept soundly with her head against his right leg, her tiny body in a tight ball. Mackenzie lay sprawled across his chest. All three mouths were wide open, their chests rising and falling in sync.

He was such a good man. He was wonderful with the kids. He'd belatedly come through for her. He'd certainly made up for his absence in the beginning.

Why couldn't she love him? Why couldn't she forget about how Noah made her feel and give Ben a chance? What good was passion, anyway, when it only caused pain and indecision?

Ben was safe, secure and solid. That's what she needed. What the kids needed in their lives. Not an MMA fighter who threw caution and responsibility to the wind whenever he stepped inside a fight cage.

Noah's life choices didn't complement the life she wanted and needed to provide for these kids.

She watched the three of them sleep for a long moment. Ben was the better choice. Did it matter that she didn't love him the way she longed for Noah?

CHAPTER TWELVE

"So, what are you going to do about the bed-and-breakfast?" Lindsay asked Victoria as she checked Harper's weight the following week at the clinic. It had been almost two months since it had shut its doors to guests and Lindsay wasn't sure if the new mom was in any rush to reopen. She recorded the eight pounds on the file and handed the sleeping baby girl back to Victoria.

Victoria cuddled Harper to her chest. "I don't know. I mean, Luke and I haven't really had a lot of time to talk about it…this little princess has been dominating most of our waking hours," she said, nuzzling the baby's cheek.

Lindsay could understand that. They were adjusting to their new roles as parents. She knew what that was like. The B and B was probably the furthest thing from their minds with everything that had happened. No doubt being there stirred memories of Rachel in the new mom. Lindsay suspected Victoria's postpartum state could do without that.

"By the way, did Ben find what he was looking for the other day?"

Lindsay frowned. "Ben was at the B and B?"

The past week he'd been working more hours. He seemed a lot more stressed, as well, though he was still holding up his end with the kids.

The night after the MMA fight, she'd apologized for being late and part of her had wanted to tell him whatever had been going on with Noah was over. But for some reason she hadn't been able to say the words out loud. In her own mind they'd sounded too final... Even though it really was the end, the words had been impossible to say.

True to form, Ben had simply nodded, smiled and kissed her forehead before saying good-night. No questions. No judgments. No anger. He made it so much harder that she wasn't attracted to him the way he was to her.

"Yeah, he said he was looking for a few of

Nathan's files." Victoria slid the baby back into her pink onesie.

"Oh…" Odd he wouldn't have mentioned it. Then again, the company had nothing to do with her.

"He said they had been working on a few deals or something."

"Of course… I'm sure he got what he needed," she said. The two men had been business partners. The company was Ben's now.

"Speaking of, are you sure you don't want any of their furniture? If not, I was planning to have Goodwill come and take the items before we reopen and turn the living quarters into more guest rooms."

She hesitated. She still needed to replace her white leather couch with something else. Something more comfortable if Ben stuck around much longer.

He hadn't talked about going back to Newark anytime soon and sleeping on her current sofa couldn't be comfortable. Maybe she should turn the dining room she never used into another bedroom.

"Maybe I'll stop by after work, if that's okay and have a look."

"Sure." Victoria reached into her purse for the keys to the B and B. "You can leave these in our mailbox at home if we're not there when you get back," she said, securing the baby in her seat.

"Thanks." She pocketed the key as she opened the exam room door. "'Bye, Harper," she said, waving at the little girl as she woke, her bright blue eyes sparkling underneath long, blond eyelashes.

Luke Dawson sure made cute babies, she thought wryly.

Three hours later Lindsay unlocked the door to the bed-and-breakfast. She gathered the old newspapers on the step and carried them inside. It felt eerie when she closed the front door behind her. The place was dark, the curtains drawn, and it smelled stale because the air conditioner had been turned off weeks before.

A cover of dust on the tables made it seem as though the inn had been abandoned for years not just a few months.

The silence made her acutely aware that she was alone. It gave her goose bumps and she shivered.

She was being silly; it was just the B and B.

She forced herself to climb the stairs toward the living quarters, but when her foot landed on the creaky step, third from the bottom, her heart nearly stopped as it echoed in the empty house.

Get a grip. That step has always squeaked.

She ran the rest of the way and, avoiding the bedrooms, which were now nearly empty, she made it to Nathan's office.

She'd never been in this room before and she felt her brother all around her. The plain maple desk and matching bookshelf he'd no doubt ordered from Ikea and assembled himself in the interest of saving money, the multicolored stacking trays from the dollar store on his desk that still held client files. And the pegboard on the wall pinned with building codes, she assumed, and several blueprints he'd been working on.

Practical and functional, just like Nathan.

His drafting table in the corner was two side-by-side ironing boards. She shook her head.

She quickly leafed through the files on his desk...work stuff. She opened the drawers, but again they were filled with company information: invoices, contract files, nothing personal.

Noticing a two-drawer file cabinet under the desk, she tried the drawers, but they were empty. She scanned the bookshelves next but found nothing.

Sitting back in his uncomfortable, cheap office chair, she closed her eyes. Her brother couldn't even have left her a sticky note with "good luck" written on it? Something? Anything? Had they really grown that far apart as adults? As children they'd been close. They had been there for one another...

"Stay in here and be quiet, okay?" she'd told him when he was four, before shutting the closet door under the staircase in their family home. She remembered creeping back to the kitchen to get her homework.

That's when the sound of plates shattering on the kitchen floor had stopped her.

"Lindsay!"

She remembered her mother's high-pitched yell as if she'd heard it this morning. Still it gave her goose bumps, just as it had when she'd been a child, slowly stepping over shards of glass in her stockinged feet.

Her mother had never allowed shoes in the house.

"Where's your brother?" Her mother's cheeks had often been mascara stained, reminding Lindsay of a raccoon. Why hadn't she worn waterproof mascara when she cried so often?

"I don't know," she'd said.

She'd refused to give away the hiding spot she'd created for her brother whenever their mother segued from depressed to angry. If only her father hadn't disappeared during those days when their mom had taken her anger out on them.

What she wouldn't have given as a child to live next door with Luke Dawson and his TV-watching, board-game-playing family. Luke and his normal family.

Stupid Nathan was always earning her a smack from her mother for lying.

They'd always needed to be out of sight in times like that. Wait out the storm over at the Dawson house until their mother's mood shifted once more and she was regretful for the damage she'd created. When she'd kiss them and hug them and tell them she was sorry.

When she was even more dangerous because Nathan started to trust her again.

Lindsay never had. She'd known better.

But Nathan had never learned.

Maybe shielding him from their mother's most destructive episodes hadn't allowed him that chance. And over the years it had created a gap between them as she'd moved further away and he'd struggled harder to gain their mother's love and acceptance.

He'd grown to think of her as a pain in his side; the annoying older sister who flirted too much, lived life a little too loud.

So why on earth had he chosen her to care for his children?

"Hi, Mayor Parsons. What brings you by?" From his perch on top of the community center's picnic table, his wrapped leg hanging over the side, Noah tossed a basketball one-handed toward the netless hoop.

To his knowledge, the mayor had been inside the center twice. Once for the ceremonial opening years before and once to receive the annual thank-you dedication plaque the center offered the city for the funding to stay open each year. Since that first year, Parsons had sent his assistant to receive the honor.

Noah felt it safe to assume his presence today wasn't a good thing.

"I have a meeting here in about five minutes." Mayor Parsons hesitated, before adding, "I'm glad you're here. Can I have a minute with you first?"

Noah caught the ball from Dominic, who'd successfully scored on the rebound of his shot, then tossed it back to the boy.

"You guys keep playing, I'll be right back," he said, climbing down from the table and reaching for his crutches.

Dr. McCarthy had removed the cast set by the fight medic the week before and X-rays had showed a hairline fracture of one of the bones in his shin. The doctor expected a full recovery in about a week.

Thank God. He had a fight in two weeks.

He followed the mayor inside, where the lack of air-conditioning made the place

smell stale and ten degrees hotter than outside. The floor fans didn't do much to ven-
tilate the space in the August heat and all of
the indoor activities and programs had been
moved outside, leaving the place empty.

Noah propped the door open to try to
force a cross-draft with the open windows.
"What's going on?" he asked.

"Noah, my office recently received appeal
applications for funding for the Turnaround
program..."

"That's right."

He'd signed and couriered them himself
the week before. Was the mayor here to personally deliver good news?

"I'm sorry to say I'm not able to reconsider it at this time."

"But, sir—"

He held up a hand, his Rolex sliding down
his arm as his suit jacket fell back.

The cost of the watch would fund the program for a year, Noah couldn't help but think.
He didn't deny the mayor the status and pay-
check years of hard work had brought him,
but the guy always seemed to forget that the

town's best interest was supposed to be his priority.

There were rumors he was hoping to run for a larger office the following year, which might explain his lack of commitment to the small town's affairs. He saw Brookhollow as a stepping stone, a launch pad to something better.

That was fine with Noah. He wanted a mayor who took local responsibilities seriously.

"It's not just this program…all community center program funding is being cut," Parsons continued.

"What? But how can these programs serve the community without government support?"

"Unfortunately they can't." Parsons checked his watch quickly. "Noah, this land is under consideration for development."

He clenched his hands at his sides. "You're closing the community center?"

"Not yet… Nothing has been decided. We just started exploring this new opportunity."

"Would you be building a new one somewhere else?"

"We don't have the money for that, no."

"What about the programs these kids rely on?"

"If we decide to go ahead with this redevelopment, some of them will be moved to the library and the schools… Others will regrettably be forced to shut down."

"Shut down. Just like that?"

"I'm afraid so. Yes. However, the majority of the funding will be recycled back into the community. Look, Noah, I'll be honest with you—I'm not completely on board with this idea. So far, I'm just taking a look at the possibility."

Mayor Parsons checked his watch at the sound of a car pulling onto the gravel parking lot. "That's my appointment."

Noah followed him outside, leaning on his crutches for support. He stopped short when he saw Ben Walker. He was the developer meeting the mayor about the land?

"Hi, Mayor Parsons," Ben said, extending a hand. "Hey, Noah." His expression was hard when their gazes met.

Noah looked between the two men. "It's your company that wants this land?" Harper Walker Developments was involved in this?

Ben glanced at the mayor. "It's confidential…"

"That's right, Noah," the mayor said. "I only told you because of your involvement with these programs. Thought you had the right to know why your funding was being denied. Please keep it to yourself until we can arrange a town meeting in a few days."

He nodded, his anger rising. He turned to Ben, giving him his coldest, hardest stare. "Was Nathan involved in this?" He couldn't believe the father of five would have been in support of buying out the land to put up… what? New condos?

Clearly this was Ben's idea and, he suspected, the main reason the guy had showed up in the guise of wanting to help Lindsay with the kids.

Ben ignored the question, instead turning to the Mayor. "Shall we?"

The Mayor nodded and the two men went inside, leaving Noah fuming outside alone.

LINDSAY'S CELL PHONE rang as she carried her grocery bags in from the minivan. It was the generic ring tone, not the specific ones she'd applied to family and friends. Telemarketers no doubt.

She sighed, balancing the bags on one arm and digging around in her purse for the phone. Just in case it was actually important...

Nathan's lawyer's number lit up her Call Display screen. Again.

She'd been meaning to call them, but it had repeatedly slipped her mind.

"Hello?" She set the bags on the porch.

"Lindsay Harper?" a man asked.

"Yes," she said.

"Have I caught you at a bad time?"

"If you were hoping for a good time, those moments are few and far between these days...so go ahead. Now's as good a time as any."

"Okay, um, this is Neil Marcus from the Henderson Law Group in Newark. We spoke a few weeks ago regarding your brother's will."

"I remember."

"Great. Well, I'm calling about your brother's business."

Disappointment seeped in. "Oh, well, I

don't have much to do with that. You'd better speak with Ben Walker, his partner."

She picked up her bags again and carried them inside, the phone propped against her shoulder. If she'd known what the call was about, she would have ignored it. The business was the last thing she needed to concern herself with. Ben seemed to be handling it fine.

"No. It's you I need. Have you had time to review the documents I gave you regarding the transfer of ownership?"

"I'm not sure what you're talking about."

"You haven't read them?"

She didn't even recall seeing them. "No."

"Nathan listed Melissa Harper as the primary co-owner of the company, but in the event that she wasn't interested, the funds from the sale of a buyout option were to be divided among all five children equally."

Funds from the sale of a buyout?

"What are you saying? The kids are still quite young. Melissa is nine. Is the company being bought out?"

"Well, that's one option. But for now, as

the primary caregiver of the children, that decision rests with you."

"Me?"

"Yes. As of right now, you effectively co-own Harper Walker Developments with Ben Walker."

She dropped the phone.

"So, THE COMPANY is yours?" Lily asked as she fed Mackenzie in her high chair.

True to form, all she'd had to do was text her friend and Lily was there.

Lindsay wiped Abigail's face with a napkin as spaghetti dripped from her chin. "Half of it, I guess." She'd searched everywhere for the documents the lawyer said he'd given her, but she hadn't found them.

"And the other half is Ben's?"

Lindsay nodded, annoyed all over again. He must have known…yet he hadn't told her. Why? Was it because he thought she'd already known? In which case, wasn't it something they should have discussed by now?

She sighed. It was all too confusing. Until she met with Neil Marcus to go over the paperwork, she really didn't understand what it all meant.

"Do you think that's the reason he showed up? To figure out why you weren't turning to him for advice about your shared company?"

Lily scraped the bottom of the bowl with the plastic Dora spoon and fed the last mouthful to the little girl, who was wearing more than she'd consumed.

Lindsay remembered what Victoria had said about Ben being in Nathan's office at the B and B. He had been there for something. But was that the case? Had he come to Brookhollow to see what control she would exercise over the business? Was he sticking around to make sure she didn't find out? Her head hurt.

"I really don't know. I mean he's been a big help around here and I'd hate to think everything he's done was to protect his own interests in his company…but…"

"But?" Lily urged.

"Vic did mention something about him stopping by the B and B to go through—"

The front door opened.

"Is that him?" Lily whispered.

They both stopped moving as if they'd been caught doing something wrong. Even the girls paused.

What was the matter with them? This was her house. She collected the girls' empty bowls and carried them to the sink, tossing Lily a washcloth. She headed into the hallway and smacked face-first into Noah's solid chest.

"Whoa..."

She placed her hands against his pectoral muscles under his form-fitting gray T-shirt to steady herself, and the effect only made her feel tipsy. They hadn't spoken since the night of his fight and his sudden appearance in her house evoked mixed feelings. "Hi," she said. "What are you—?"

"Why didn't you tell me the real reason Ben's here?" he demanded, his expression hard as he readjusted his crutches under his arms.

She frowned. Had he heard her and Lily talking moments before? She'd only gotten the call from Nathan's lawyer a few hours ago. "What do you mean?"

His eyes narrowed. "We need to talk," he said, dragging her away from the kitchen, out of earshot of Lily and the girls.

"Hey!" She yanked her arm away. "This is my house and we are in the middle of dinner. Can't this wait?"

Any happiness she may have felt at seeing him had vanished.

"Just tell me. Did you know about the community center?"

Noah rested his forearms on his crutches, studying her intently.

Smiling, he was gorgeous. But serious and annoyed, Noah was downright swoonworthy.

"What about it?"

"It's under consideration for land development." He paused, waiting.

Her eyes widened and she shook her head. "No way. Ben wouldn't do that."

Would he?

Lily's theory was starting to sound more plausible by the second.

Lindsay's stomach turned.

Noah's expression darkened. "I'm sorry

to tell you, but you may not know your boyfriend as well as you think you do."

"He's not my boyfriend. He's..." What was he? He'd been staying with her for almost a month. Taking care of the kids.

"Look, whatever you two have going on is none of my business," he said, jealousy seeping from his tone as he ran a hand over his short, dark hair. "But the community center is my business. Where is he?"

Noah glanced into the living room.

"I don't know. But how do you know all of this?"

There had to be a mistake. Ben and Nathan worked together on all major projects. And there was no way Nathan would have considered destroying something as important to Brookhollow as the community center.

"He met with Mayor Parsons today at the center."

"And they told you? They actually said the center is being torn down?"

She bit her lip, her newfound knowledge that she now owned part of her brother's company burning in her mind.

She wished she'd never answered the phone earlier today.

"The Mayor said they were just in discussion about it right now…" He sighed, running a hand through his hair.

Good, nothing was for sure yet. "Noah, I may be able to help," she said slowly. "Emphasis on *may*," she added quickly, not wanting to get his hopes up.

The lawyer had said she was currently the co-owner, so she would have a say in decisions such as this, wouldn't she? And if Noah was finding out about it today, surely they had time to stop it from happening.

"How?"

"Well, apparently I own part of the company now…or at least the children do or Melissa does… I don't know all the details yet."

Immediately he crossed the room as fast as he could on crutches. "You can stop this deal? That would be fantastic."

His excitement and relief only made her cringe. "Hang on. I don't know. I have no idea how much say I have."

"As partner, you would have to sign off on this." He nodded. "Yeah, I'm sure of it…"

She released a deep sigh. *A heads-up about all of this would have been fantastic, Nathan*, she thought. Of course her brother had never expected things to turn out the way they had. He may have prepared for such a circumstance, but no one ever believed it would actually happen.

"I'll talk to Ben."

Noah brought her hand to his lips and placed a quick kiss on her palm. "Thank you. I'm not sure how many more of the things I care about I can lose to Ben Walker."

"IT'S YOUR TURN, Aunt Lindsay," Jacob said, waving a tiny hand in front of her face as her gaze once again drifted out the window, looking for Ben's vehicle in the driveway.

She turned her attention back to the board game. "Right, sorry." She spun the spinner, landed on five and moved her Disney character six spaces.

"Hey, cheater, that's six," Caleb said, moving her game piece back one space.

"Sorry, guys. I'm a little distracted right now. Can we play later?"

"We need three players," Jacob said, taking his turn.

Lindsay glanced toward Melissa on the nearby sofa, watching *Gossip Girl*. "Maybe your sister will play."

Melissa shook her head. "No way, they cheat."

"No, we don't. Not since we were little kids," Caleb argued, frowning.

"Right, because you're not a little kid anymore." Melissa rolled her eyes.

"You're only a few years older than us," Jacob said, standing to block her view of the television.

"Move, brat!" she yelled as Caleb joined his brother to dance and block her view of the screen. "Aunt Lindsay, I'm going to kill them, I swear," Melissa said, jumping up off of the couch and rushing them.

"Hey, don't touch me!" Jacob shouted.

"Na-nan-a-boo-boo," Caleb chanted, running away from her.

Lindsay's head throbbed. "Hey, guys! Quit it," she said, louder and more angry than she'd intended.

Where was Ben?

All three kids paused to look at her in surprise.

"Sorry. Please keep it down and, boys, stop bugging your sister."

"I'm going to finish watching this in my room," Melissa said, disappearing down the hall and slamming her door shut.

Lindsay cringed. That door was coming off the hinges the closer that girl got to her teen years.

The boys sat back down at the game. "She's no fun anymore," Jacob said.

The sound of the Land Rover doors locking outside made her jump. He was here.

"Okay, guys, I need you to go play in your room, okay? Bath time is in half an hour," she said, sliding the game pieces off the board and into the box, struggling to close the lid. These things never went back in the way they came out. Giving up, she handed the box to Caleb. "Here you go," she said as the front door opened.

Lindsay met Ben in the hall.

"Hey. Sorry I—"

"Don't worry about it." She cut him off. "We need to talk."

He removed his shoes and she took in his dark gray, pin-striped suit and his white dress shirt open at the collar. He had a dark blue tie in his hand.

"I take it you spoke to Noah," he said shortly.

She couldn't decide if he seemed annoyed because she obviously knew about the community center or just because she'd spoken to Noah. It didn't matter, she decided. What mattered was that it appeared Ben had been conducting business that day.

"He said Harper Walker Developments is shutting down the community center."

Ben went into the kitchen and took a bottle of water out of the fridge, opening it. He took a sip before answering. "Technically, the town may be shutting down the community center. The company is interested in buying the land."

"Semantics," she mumbled. "So it's really happening?"

"I don't know yet. The first meeting with the Mayor went well."

Went well? He thought buying the land and shutting down one of the town's landmarks was a good thing? "I can't believe you."

"Lindsay, I know the community center is important…"

"Obviously not. And why didn't you mention this to me? I am part owner of the company now." She waited for his reaction.

He didn't looked surprised that she knew. "I was planning to talk to you about it tonight." He slumped into the armchair by the window and his gaze settled on something in the distance.

He sighed. "Lindsay, the truth is, the company isn't doing well. For the last six months, Nathan and I were struggling and we couldn't agree on almost anything." He paused. "I first mentioned this opportunity to him a year ago when I was approached by a contractor interested in the land for a new strip mall."

A strip mall? They wanted to tear down a community center for a shopping outlet? Unbelievable.

"I tried to convince myself the jobs the new mall would provide here outweighed the benefits of the community center. But this was *Nathan's* town, not mine, and it was impossible to convince him of that."

"You won't convince me, either. There are

so many great programs at that community center." She placed her palms on the table.

"I know."

"Really? Then why would you reconsider this option now that my brother is gone?"

"Because this deal could save the company."

"Didn't you hear me? The community center is *important* to Brookhollow. My brother was right about this and I'm not backing down, Ben. Besides, you need my signature on it, don't you?"

She held her breath at his wide-eyed expression. She had no idea if he did or not.

He stood and moved toward her, frustration in his eyes. "Let me ask you something—and be honest."

"Okay." She placed her hands on her hips and waited.

"Is this really about saving the community center or is it about Noah?"

Her mouth dropped.

Could these two ever get it through their thick skulls that not everything was about them?

"Noah was the one who told me, but this is not about him," she said firmly.

"Are you sure about that? Because this deal will make sure that all five of those kids have the best opportunities in life. Their college will be paid for and you'll never have to worry about their futures."

She was about to argue, but she couldn't think what to say to that.

"Nathan may have been reluctant to put his family's future ahead of the needs of the community, but I'm not."

CHAPTER THIRTEEN

"NOAH IS STILL in the waiting room," Rebecca said, poking her head around the lunch room door.

Lindsay didn't glance up from the three-month-old issue of *Vogue* she'd already read cover to cover. "So? Take him in."

"He asked to see you."

Of course he did. He'd called twice and texted three times since the day before. Each time she saw his number light up her phone, a heavy weight had crushed her and she'd continued to ignore him. "Tell him I'm not available to chat."

"Tell me yourself. Unless you're not done avoiding me," he said, appearing in the doorway behind Rebecca.

"This lunchroom is for staff only," she said through gritted teeth, a memory of the last time they'd been in there together making her cheeks flame.

"That didn't stop us before," he said purposely with a smirk.

Rebecca's eyes widened as she glanced between the two of them.

Fantastic. Now rumors would spread that something had happened between them in the clinic's lunchroom. Of course, something *had* happened. She'd fallen in love with him.

"Fine," she said, closing the magazine, standing and pushing them both out into the hallway. "Follow me," she said to Noah, leading the way into the farthest exam room at the back of the clinic, away from Rebecca's ears.

Once she closed the door behind them, she turned to face him. "I haven't been avoiding you."

"What would you call three unanswered text messages and two unreturned calls?"

"Busy. I have a life, Noah."

"I know you have a life. One you don't want me to be a part of. I get that. I don't like it. But I get it. But I need to know what's going on with the center because it's one of the few things I have left to care about these days."

She swallowed the lump in her throat. "I'm not sure I can help save the center," she said quietly.

His forehead creased. "Why not? If Ben is telling you he can do this without your cooperation, he's lying."

"He's not. He admitted he needs my signature."

She stared at the scuffed tiled floor at her feet, unable to meet his gaze. How could she look at him when she was about to tell him she could save the community center if she tried—she just wouldn't? He was going to hate her.

"So what's the problem? Don't sign."

Sure, because life was just that easy, she thought bitterly.

"Noah, it's complicated."

"You're kidding, right? You actually think a strip mall is better for the community than a center for kids…a center your own kids benefit from."

No. Even though she'd been trying to convince herself of that all day.

"The jobs the stores will create will be appreciated." That much was true at least. And, really, the only benefit to all this. The one she was desperately clinging to…to ease her guilty conscience. "I mean, look at Play Hard," she continued quickly. "No one saw the value of that store, either, until Victoria convinced them otherwise, and look how great it's been for so many people."

"This is hardly the same thing. Legend's Sporting Goods wasn't helping anyone. And besides, Luke turned it into a museum. You can't compare the two, Lindsay."

She wished he wasn't right. She sighed, busying herself with his chart. "Well, it appears that the bone is setting nicely…" She carefully kept her voice void of the emotional extremes she was feeling.

He advanced toward her, taking the file from her and forcing her to look at him. "What is with you? Yesterday you were on my side. What changed?"

"A quarter of a million dollars changed." There she'd said it. Now he could hate her.

"Money?"

"Yes, money!" Her hands gestured frantically as she spoke quickly. "I'm a nurse Noah…and suddenly I have the future of five little people to consider. Kids whose father started this venture to make sure they were set for anywhere life took them. How do I deny them the future he'd worked so hard to secure?"

It had taken hours after her talk with Ben for the realization of what he'd said to sink in.

This deal was worth half a million dollars to the company and would give them more opportunity to grow. After a heavy-hearted, sleepless night, she'd decided she would do what her brother had fought against. Nathan may have been confident that the company would succeed without this deal and he would be able to provide the best life for his children, but she wasn't as sure of herself.

"Things change. That much you should know better than anyone. And, besides, you have a million years before these kids go to university—if they choose to. You can't base decisions—major decisions—now on what could happen in the future."

She felt her heart harden. This was exactly why she hadn't been able to let go and trust Noah. The very reason she'd pushed him away.

He lived in the here-and-now—carefree to the point of recklessness in his choices. He had no plans for a future if his fighting career didn't work, or worse, left him injured so badly someday that his own future was jeopardized. So, how could she ever trust him to think about a future with her, a future for the kids, when here he was telling her not to worry about it?

"You care about those kids at the center. I understand that. So do I. But I have to do what's right for the ones that matter most to me. I'm sorry, Noah, but I'm signing the deal."

She took back his file and pretended to read it, but the words swam together on the page as tears filled her eyes. She furiously blinked them away.

Stay strong. At least for a few more minutes.

He was silent for an excruciatingly long moment and when she finally found the strength to meet his gaze, his expression was hurt and betrayed. "Well then, I guess you're not the person I thought you were, after all."

After everything she'd been through the past few months, she hadn't thought it possible to achieve yet another level of sorrow. It turned out she was wrong.

Squaring her jaw, she forced her voice to remain steady as she said, "People are who they are, Noah. And if you can't accept that, walk away."

"Walk away," he repeated and nodded slowly. "Like you did?"

"Like I did."

Without another word, he moved past her for the door and, swinging it open, left the room.

"I CAN'T BELIEVE Lindsay refuses to stop this," Ethan said as he turned the fire truck into the community center parking lot.

"Me, either," he grumbled. He understood wanting to do the best thing for her kids, but at what cost to so many other people? His disappointment over the potential loss of the program was overshadowed by his disappointment in Lindsay and her unwillingness to help.

"I'm sorry, man," Ethan said, tapping him on the shoulder. "But the good news is that we have a full-time spot on the team coming up with Mark Adams leaving next month. It's yours if you want it. Save lives in a different way…or at least rescue cats from trees and get paid for a change."

Noah nodded. "Thanks, Ethan. I appreciate the offer. If I win my next fight, I may not have time, even for my volunteer role."

He planned to focus all his energy on his fighting—the one thing he had control over and the one thing in his life he could depend on.

"I totally get it. I'd choose a career in MMA over firefighting any day…if my wife would let me." He laughed as he put the truck in Park.

"Of course she'd let you. Bailey loves MMA. You should have seen her at my fight."

Ethan rolled his eyes. "Yes, I saw the countless photos she took that night."

His tone reflected the slightest jealousy and it was hard to tell if he was jealous because she'd attended the fights without him or because of all of the photos of her and the MMA fighters.

"The thing is, she loves to watch other guys fight. Even her brothers—although she's happy they stick to coaching. It's one thing to watch strangers fight, it's totally different when you watch someone you care about. She'd never want me to fight."

"Yeah, I guess. Anyway, thanks for the ride." He jumped down from the truck and tossed his duffel bag over one shoulder.

The sound of a police siren at the back of the building made him frown. Going around the side, he saw a Brookhollow squad car park and the new Sherriff get out. He'd seen the man around the fire hall that shared the building with the police station and he'd been at the hospital the night of the accident, but he'd yet to formally meet the man.

It looked as if he was about to.

He shielded his eyes from the glare of the car's flashing lights. "Hey, what's going on?" Was he putting cuffs on someone?

"Stay back, please," Sherriff Matthews

said. When he turned, Noah saw that the kid in front of him was Dominic.

"Hey," he said, ignoring the man and moving closer. "That's one of my kids. What are you doing?"

"I said stay back," the officer said with more force this time.

Noah stopped. This guy was intense.

"Sorry, I won't come any closer, but can you explain to me what's happening."

Dominic stared at the ground, refusing to speak as his hands were cuffed behind him. He looked guilty as anything.

What did you do, Dominic?

"Are you his father?" the young officer asked.

"No. His mentor here at the center." Not for long, he thought grimly.

"Great job," the other man said sarcastically, and Noah stiffened. "Well, I guess you at least taught him to spell properly."

Noah's eyes narrowed. Who was this jerk? "What are you talking about?"

The officer kicked a can of spray paint and it rolled to Noah's feet.

He picked it up and glanced at the building. The words *Mayor Parsons Sucks* were written in dark green across the side of the building.

As much as he had to agree with the bold statement, his heart sank. "Dominic. You did this?"

"Of course he did. I caught him doing it," the officer said.

"I'm talking to the kid," Noah said. "Dominic?"

Dominic nodded.

Great. Noah sighed. "Are the handcuffs necessary? It's a can of spray paint, not a knife."

"This time," Sherriff Matthews muttered, but he removed the cuffs. "Don't go anywhere," he said to Dominic.

The kid rubbed his wrists. "What were you thinking?" Noah demanded.

"They're planning to tear it down anyway," Dominic mumbled.

Huh, maybe telling the boy that there was a chance of that hadn't been such a great idea, after all, but he'd been so upset about the program possibly being shut down, Noah had needed to be honest with him. He didn't want the boy thinking it was because he'd given up. "Vandalism is a punishable offense and you've insulted the mayor."

"What I wrote is true. Everyone thinks so."

Noah couldn't exactly argue the point. "Regardless, this is not acceptable." He turned to Sherriff Matthews. "This is the first time this boy has ever done anything like this…and he's upset."

He prayed Dominic wasn't getting the wrong idea about his plea to the cop. He wasn't off the hook for this. Not even close. But he hoped the officer wouldn't insist on filing criminal charges against him. Not when the boy had just filled out college applications.

"I still need to take him in."

Wow, he was going to be a wonderful addition to the community. Who hired him anyway?

"What if Dominic agrees to remove this right away and perform some community service? Can we put this to rest now instead of taking him in?"

"That's not protocol," the guy said. Noah caught a thick New York accent.

That explained a lot. Except for why a New York City cop wanted the low-paying, low-action job of deputy sheriff in a town of less than ten thousand residents. "I understand, but this is Brookhollow, not New York. I think you'll find that most things don't go according to protocol around here. It's called giving people a chance."

"A chance? To do what? Become better criminals?"

Noah's jaw tensed. "I assure you, that's not always the case."

The officer hesitated then shook his head. "Whatever. I want this off the building by tomorrow morning." He turned to Dominic. "If I catch you with a spray can or anything else in your hand doing damage again, you won't get off so easy. Got it?"

Dominic nodded.

They watched Deputy-Sheriff Matthews get back in his car, cut the flashing lights and drive away.

"What a moron," Dominic mumbled next to him.

Again, Noah couldn't really disagree.

"What is this?" he asked, turning to gesture toward the wall. "Are you freaking kidding me? You're lucky I was here or you would have this stunt on your permanent record for the next seven years."

Dominic shrugged. "It was a joke."

"Not funny. Stupid. This could affect your chances of getting into college."

The boy looked away.

"Tell me you mailed those applications we filled out."

Dominic nodded. "Yeah."

"Don't lie to me."

"I'm not," he said. "I sent them."

Noah struggled with whether or not to believe him. Ten minutes ago he'd never have thought the kid would pull a stupid stunt like this. "Okay. Let's go get something to remove this."

"You're going to help?"

"No way. You do the crime, you do the time."

The kid stopped on the way to Noah's motorcycle. "Do you really think they are going to tear the place down?"

Noah let out a deep breath to the darkening sky. "I hope not." There was still a chance to have his voice and opinion heard at the town meeting the next evening and he was pretty sure he wouldn't be the only one fighting to prevent the center from being torn down.

He just wished the one person who could actually stop this deal was on his side.

CHAPTER FOURTEEN

SITTING IN THE back of the town hall's meeting room the following evening, Lindsay hunched in the plastic chair as Mayor Parsons took the podium. She wasn't sure who else in the room knew why this town meeting had been called but she knew once everyone found out they weren't going to be happy. She wasn't happy about it, either, but being an immediate recipient to its benefits, people were hardly going to believe she was as much opposed to the center's demolition as they were.

Noah sat in the front row. He was wearing a pair of dress pants and a dress shirt and tie. The same tie she remembered teasing him about at Bailey and Ethan's wedding several months before.

Only several months? It felt like a lifetime since she'd loosened that tie and narrowly averted his lips as he'd tried to kiss her. If only she could go back to a time when she didn't know how his kisses felt.

Noah's knees bounced and he turned to scan the quickly crowding room. She averted her gaze but not quickly enough and the coldness in his made her shiver. So different from the look he'd given her a few days ago. When he thought she could stop this. *Would* stop this.

You're not the person I thought you were.

She stared at her hands as several people she didn't recognize moved past her into the row and sat.

"Hello, everyone," Mayor Parsons started. "Thank you all for coming. As many of you have known for years, our younger generation is moving away in search of jobs and better opportunities that unfortunately Brookhollow can't provide…but we are hoping to change that. Similar to the employment opportunities Play Hard Sports has provided, there's a new opportunity for development of a new strip mall in town."

He paused.

A murmur of conversation rippled through the crowd and Lindsay cringed. Sure, Mayor

Parsons, tell them the good news first, get their hopes up that this is a good thing.

She felt nauseous.

"Of course, as many of you also know, the land around the community center has been government property since the late eighties…and we are considering its use for the development of this new venture," he said.

The murmurs died down and silence fell over the room for a moment before hands went up and people began to bombard him.

Mayor Parsons held up a hand. "We are open to questions, but please, one at a time."

Delores Myers stood. "What does that mean for the community center?"

The question on everyone's mind, it seemed, as most raised hands lowered and everyone stared at the mayor.

"Unfortunately, it does mean the center would be torn down," he said.

More whispers and murmurs, disbelief, all around her. She closed her eyes.

Pat Morry, a father of four, who owned a convenience store in town, stood. "Will the city be rebuilding the center somewhere else?"

Lindsay held her breath. If that was the plan, it would help ease the guilt she was feeling.

"No," Mayor Parsons answered.

She blew her breath out between her lips.

"Will the center's programs be held somewhere else?" asked Mrs. Mason, Victoria's mother.

Lindsay ran her hand through her hair as the mayor shook his head.

"The government funding now allocated to those programs would, however, be transferred to local school programs and the library."

"What about town events?" Darlene Dawson said as she stood, looking more than ready to fight.

"We could hold them elsewhere."

"Great. I assume your home's available?" she said and a snicker ran through the crowd.

Good for you, Mrs. Dawson. The mayor's four-thousand-square-foot home was the biggest in Brookhollow and it was no secret he held high-society events there frequently— although few residents ever received an invitation.

He smiled tightly. "The school gymnasium would be a suitable substitution, I think, and during the summer, fund-raising events could be held at the park." He turned his attention to the crowd. "I realize this change would affect a lot of you and it may be hard to see the benefits—"

"I'd like to speak if I could," Noah said, standing.

The mayor frowned then slowly nodded. "Of course. Everyone's voice is welcome," he said tightly.

Noah moved to the center at the front of the room.

Lindsay stared at him, aching for the man. Everything he'd worked so hard to achieve for the kids...

She'd heard about Dominic's vandalism. It broke her heart to think of all the kids like Dominic who'd been doing so well under Noah and the other volunteers' guidance and support.

He cleared his throat. "Unlike a lot of you, I haven't been in Brookhollow long, so it's probably surprising to see me standing here. For those of you I haven't met, I'm Noah and

I run the Turnaround program at the community center."

A round of applause made him pause. He lowered his head and she noticed his cheeks redden. "Thank you. The Turnaround program helped eight kids secure employment this year. It's helped even more graduate high school. These kids need this program." He picked up a stack of papers from his chair and started handing them out. "These are the pictures and stories of every kid we've reached…and on the back is a petition to save the community center, to save this program and all the others the kids have learned to depend on."

When he noticed her, Noah's stone-cold stare pinned Lindsay like a mosquito to a pegboard and her mouth went dry.

She stood and grabbed her purse, rushing to the door and holding her breath until she was outside.

"Lindsay!"

"Noah, I'm sorry."

"You're running out of here, walking away from this as if it's not your problem. I get it." He handed her a copy of his petition and she glanced at the kids' bios and pictures. Her eyes watered. "But, at least take a look at the kids the community center has helped and those who still rely on this support."

"Noah, this isn't an easy thing for me, okay? As you said inside, you didn't grow up here—I did. That center holds memories for me. Good ones, great ones."

"But even that's not enough to change your mind, so I don't have a hope in trying." He shrugged. "I should have learned by now there's no changing your mind about anything."

She watched him climb the stairs to go back inside.

Her feet remained frozen to the spot.

Brookhollow may need the community center...but her family needed this deal.

LINDSAY MARCHED INTO Brent's Dodge early the next morning, the invoice for the mini-van repairs she'd received from Bailey's Place in her hand. "I need to see Doug," she said to the dealership's receptionist.

"Doug Miller? Or Doug Cooper?" she asked.

She hesitated. What was the man's last name again? "Whichever one is the biggest con artist," Lindsay said.

"Ah, Doug Cooper. One second," the young woman said, dialing the used-car manager. "Doug C to reception. Customer waiting." She set the phone down. "He'll be here in a minute."

Lindsay checked her watch. She had an hour before her shift started at the clinic, but she needed a reliable vehicle for her and the kids, not the piece of crap this dealership had tried to pawn off on the clueless blonde.

Bailey had been apologetic that morning when she'd emailed her the invoice for the work she'd done on the minivan weeks before, but this wasn't Bailey's fault. Still, the thousand-dollar invoice was one Lindsay couldn't exactly afford to pay.

Ten minutes later, giving her plenty of time to get even more upset, Doug walked through the main dealership's front doors, wearing his signature black dress pants and dealership windbreaker. It was ninety degrees outside, yet the man wasn't even sweating. No doubt lack of body fat kept him running cool all the time.

Well, he'd be sweating bullets in a minute if she had anything to do with it.

"Hi, Lindsay!"

"You sold me a lemon," she replied loudly.

Several customers in the showroom stopped to look in their direction. She didn't care if she was bad for business. People should know what they were really buying here.

Doug's smile faded. "Uh, why don't we head over to my office?"

"No. Let's talk here. That piece of crap minivan broke down less than a month after I bought it and now I have an invoice for a thousand dollars for servicing and new parts."

She waved the invoice in front of him.

Thankfully, Bailey had been able to locate cheap parts and had charged her next to nothing for labor, or she'd be in for more than the original cost of the van.

"It's a secondhand vehicle, Lindsay, things break down. You didn't purchase the extended warranties I suggested—"

"Are you kidding me? You're hiding behind that? This is *my* fault?" Her voice rose and the general manager came out of his office.

Good. If she got nowhere with Doug, she could take this up with him.

He shot Doug a look and gestured he take this conversation elsewhere.

"Why don't we go outside and have a smoke?" he suggested, reaching into his pocket for the cigarettes.

"I quit." She folded her arms and stood firm.

"Look, our vehicles are sold as is. Now, if you'd bought the warranties I'd recommended several times, we could cover some of the maintenance costs you've incurred this month, but I'm sorry. There's not much we can do."

Buyer beware. She swallowed hard, unsure if that was it. What else could she say? She hadn't bought the warranties, but she'd trusted that the ten-year-old vehicle would last longer than it had without so many issues.

"So, that's it? You're not going to help me? You're standing behind your company policy and basically I'm screwed?" She bit the inside of her cheek. She refused to cry.

This jerk didn't deserve that satisfaction. Besides, with everything else going wrong these days, car trouble should be last on the list of things to cry about.

Doug softened. "Please, come over to my office and I'll see what I can do, okay?"

She hesitated, wondering if she should talk to the general manager instead.

"And actually, I'm glad you stopped by."

"Yeah, right."

"No, really. I mean, you're totally killing our sales department right now, but I have something in my office that belongs to you. I found it in your trade-in."

Her eyes narrowed. "I cleaned out the trade-in." She'd gone over every inch twice.

"There was a file folder that had fallen between the passenger seat and the center glove compartment. Looked to be important. And also a letter. I've been meaning to call you. Come on, I'll get it for you."

A letter? Her heart stopped.

BACK IN HER minivan ten minutes later, with a promise from Doug that the dealership would cover half her invoice costs, Lindsay placed the larger envelope containing the information regarding the company on the passenger seat and stared at the white letter-size envelope in her hand, her name on the front in Nathan's handwriting.

The explanation she'd been wanting from her brother was in her hands and she couldn't gather the strength and courage to open it.

Would it be a how-to list about how to take care of his children? That would have been helpful a few months ago. Her fears about raising them were still there, but they were motivating her to do better, to be better, to make better choices, instead of the crippling indecisions they'd once been.

Opening the envelope and unfolding the piece of paper inside, she took a deep breath. Then holding the letter with two shaking hands, she read it.

Dear Linds,
With any luck, you will never read this letter as, being the firstborn, you're supposed to die first. But somehow I think you'll outlive me anyway. I think

you'll find a way to flirt your way out of death.

I respect and admire you, even if I've never told you before. You are you—for good or bad, like it or not—you are you. When Rachel and I decided to name you legal guardian of our kids in the event of our death, we obviously hoped the day would never come, especially since we love our kids so much we couldn't stop at two or three or four… We're leaving you with five. But before you freak out, just know this—we expect you won't raise them exactly the way we would have, but I'm okay with that.

I can rest in peace knowing my children are with you for one simple reason. Above all else, you will keep them safe. And what more could a father ask for? I know this for sure because you always kept me safe.

I haven't said this in a long time… Forget it, I'm not saying it now, either, because I don't think I need to.

Be good, Linds, and just do your best. Nathan

Her breath was escaping in tiny pants as she fought to control the overwhelming emotions closing in on her. Tears flowed freely down her cheeks as she folded the letter with trembling hands and slid it back into the envelope. Hugging it to her chest, she relaxed against the seat.

"Thank you, Nathan," she whispered.

CHAPTER FIFTEEN

LINDSAY COULD BARELY keep her eyes open. Her first day back in Emergency since the accident, the twelve-hour shift feeling twice as long as normal. But she'd made it through.

A quick glance at the clock revealed two minutes left on her shift. Close enough, she thought, heading toward the staff room. When the emergency doors opened behind her a second later, she cringed. If only she could pretend not to have heard them.

Sighing, she turned.

The sight of the stretchers coming in through the doors made her heart pound and the memory of the night her brother and Rachel had been wheeled in came flooding back. She ignored the queasy feeling in her stomach and met the paramedics.

"What have we got?" she asked before

glancing at the young man on the stretcher. Oh, no. "Dominic? What happened to you?"

The boy's eyes were swollen and bruised and his nose was clearly broken. The white sheet over his body covered any other damage, but she suspected his injuries didn't stop at his face. He tried to speak but started coughing, grabbing his rib cage in pain.

Lindsay turned to the paramedics. "What happened?"

"Mrs. Dillon called 9-1-1 when she saw him limping home an hour ago. He passed out on the sidewalk across from her house."

"Okay, take him to the third room down the hall. I'll page Dr. McCarthy."

Ten minutes later Dr. McCarthy and Lindsay examined the extent of the boy's injuries. "Two broken ribs on the right side and a lot of bruising. That's all I can determine without X-rays. We'll send him right away."

On his left, Lindsay was setting his IV. "Has anyone called his mother?"

Dominic's eyes widened and he shook his head, grabbing her hand.

"What's wrong, honey?" she asked, sympathetically as she noticed tears in the teen-ager's eyes.

"Don't call her…please… Call Noah."

Lindsay swallowed hard before nodding. "Okay, I'll call Noah…but then he'll have to contact your mom, okay?"

Tears ran down the boy's face as he nodded.

Outside the examining room, Lindsay dialed Noah's number, her hand shaking slightly. They hadn't spoken since the night outside the town hall and though he'd been at the clinic earlier that day for his clearance form for his healed leg, he hadn't asked for her and she'd waited—okay, hid—in the staff room until he'd left. Calling him now, with bad news, was the last thing she felt like doing.

The phone rang once, and then went straight to voice mail. Fantastic. Now he was avoiding *her*. Not exactly good timing, Noah, she thought as she hit Redial. This time the phone didn't even ring before going straight to voice mail. She hung up and clicked on the last text message she'd received from him.

Pretty girl, stop avoiding me, it read.

Ironic.

Answer your phone, it's an emergency, she texted.

Immediately her phone rang.

"Are you okay?" he asked. The worry in his voice erased any anger she felt.

"I'm fine. It's Dominic. The paramedics—"

"I'll be right there."

"I BET TEACHING me how to fight doesn't seem like such a bad idea now, huh?" Dominic croaked through his breathing mask in the hospital bed.

Noah's stomach tightened at the sight of the teen's excessive injuries. This was more than a schoolyard bully fight. And somehow he'd known this would happen.

"Knowing how to fight doesn't always prevent injuries." He sat in the chair next to the boy's bed. "What happened?"

Dominic shrugged. "They attacked from behind. I really don't know."

"You're the worst liar I know. Want to try the truth this time?"

"It was Erik and his friends, okay?"

"Your own cousin did this to you?" He clenched his teeth.

This wasn't the first time Dominic had stood his ground against his cousin, and the deep bruising and gashes on his face, making him swollen and unrecognizable, were the price he paid.

"So, will you teach me?"

"I'll teach you how to defend yourself better. Duck and block," he said. At Dominic's small size, he barely stood a chance against the bigger boys, especially when they rarely acted alone.

"Come on, man, this is going to keep happening to me…" He rested his head against his pillow and winced in pain.

He sat forward, grateful that Lindsay waited in the hallway, as he said, "Look, I'll teach you a few basic moves, okay? Any day now I'm sure you'll get your acceptance letters to those colleges you applied to for the winter semester and be leaving Brookhollow anyway."

He wished Dominic had had enough credits to apply for the fall semester. He would have already been settled in at college and he'd have avoided this attack. If he could stay on track until December, he would be safe in a dorm room, away from his cousin, on his way to a degree and making a life for himself.

"I got them," he muttered.

"When?"

"Last week."

Noah's eyes widened. "Why didn't you tell me?" Had the boy not gotten in?

"I wanted to, but then everything with the community center happened and you had enough on your mind," he said with a cough, clutching his side.

"Well? What did they say?"

"I was accepted to all of them."

He touched the boy's shoulder. "That's great, man. Congratulations."

Dominic frowned and shrugged. "It doesn't matter. I can't go."

"Oh, you're going," Noah said with a firm nod. If he had to pack the kid up and drive him to one of the campuses himself, he would. In fact, maybe there was a way he could move him to New York or Boston or wherever he decided to go early...before the term started. Maybe he could get a part-time job for a few months before classes started. Once he was feeling better, of course.

"My student loan application was denied. I can't afford to go." Tears rimmed his eyes and he looked away.

Noah frowned. Maybe the boy hadn't filled them out correctly.

"What about the money you saved from your after-school job?" It wasn't enough to pay for the year, but the boy had worked at the hardware store in town since he was fifteen.

"It's gone."

Noah's fist clenched on his lap. "Tell me where I can find Erik," he said, his voice hard.

"No, it wasn't him. Mom's insurance ran out."

Dammit.

The boy had far too much responsibility placed on his shoulders. He had so much potential, so many opportunities ahead of him, and he was stuck. How on earth could the student loan application have been denied? The boy and his mother lived on her disability income, which was barely enough to keep a roof over their heads. If Dominic didn't qualify for student aid, who did?

Noah took a deep breath. "What happened with the loan? What was the reason they gave for denying it?"

"My dad makes too much money."

His dad? The jerk who'd left him and his mother with nothing? *That* guy. The one who paid zero in child support and hadn't seen his son in years?

Unbelievable.

How the government could even consider that income when calculating Dominic's need for additional support was baffling.

He ran a hand over his head. "Okay, well, we'll figure something else out."

"It's okay, Noah…it is what it is," he said, closing his eyes.

Noah sat back in the chair. No, he refused to accept that.

One way or another this kid was going to college.

"LINDSAY!" NOAH CALLED as he crossed the parking lot.

Lindsay turned slowly. She looked tired and disillusioned. "Is he sleeping?"

He nodded. "Yes. And his mom is here

now, so I said I'd stop by again in the morning." He shoved his hands into his jeans' pockets. "Thank you for calling me."

"He asked me to."

Right.

"Yeah, um, listen…I want to apologize for what I said the other day. About you not being—"

She held up a hand. "I remember what you said."

"I'm really sorry. I was upset." He looked away. "But it was mean and selfish and I'm sorry."

"Okay." She turned to go.

"Lindsay, please wait." He had no idea what to say; he just knew he didn't want her to walk away again angry and hurt because of him.

"Noah, it's almost midnight and I just had to care for a kid whose own cousin broke two of his ribs. I could have helped you and I didn't. So, please, whatever you have to say, save it for another time."

In two quick strides he closed the gap between them and wrapped his arms around her.

"I'm sorry, Lindsay. I really am. I was

harsh, criticizing your decision. You were doing the best thing for *your* kids… It took me until tonight to see how important that is."

He smoothed her blond curls down her back.

"If more parents cared about their children as much as you do those kids, we wouldn't need programs or community centers. They would feel safe and loved at home."

"But we do need those places. Dominic needs those places…" She buried her face in his chest and her body sagged against him.

"You're doing what's right for your family and no one can blame you for that. I'm sorry I did." He moved back and lifted her chin, forcing her to look into his eyes. "And I'm sorry about something else, too."

"What?" she whispered.

"This." His lips claimed hers and he pulled her into him, tightening his hold on her hips.

She kissed him back and the connection was angry and sad and full of passion at the same time. All he cared about at that moment was holding her, kissing her.

Reluctantly, she stepped back. "I have to go."

He nodded. She did have to go—before he could no longer let her go.

Now more than ever, he needed his fighting career.

LINDSAY PACED THE hallway outside the bathroom door the next morning, listening to the running water of the shower. Come on, Ben. The man took the longest showers of anyone she knew. She checked her watch.

The water shut off and she heard the shower curtain being pulled back. She leaned against the wall opposite the bathroom door and waited. More water…the buzz of his electric toothbrush… Maybe she should let the man get ready in peace and wait for him in the kitchen.

She knocked on the door.

"Hello?" came his reply.

"It's me. I need to talk to you."

Her hands shook slightly. She wasn't sure what his reaction would be, but she didn't care.

A moment later he opened the door in his

jeans and T-shirt, hopping on one foot as he pulled on a sock. "Everything okay?"

"No." She took a deep breath. "I can't go through with this deal. I need you to reconsider."

He put on his other sock silently and she waited. And waited.

"Ben, please." That's it. Now she would shut up. She clamped her lips tightly.

"I guess you haven't had coffee yet." He moved past her into the hall and started for the kitchen.

She huffed. "Don't patronize me. I don't need coffee to think clearly." She paused when he shot a glance over his shoulder. "Okay, most days I do...but not about this. I've made up my mind, Ben. I'm canceling this deal."

"You can't," he said, turning the corner.

She followed quickly, her blood running cold. "What do you mean?"

He hit the button on the coffeemaker. Opening the cupboard, he took down her favorite mug. "Why don't you sit?"

"I don't want to sit. I need us to go to the mayor's office downtown and tell him we're not interested."

"Lindsay, please sit." He sat at the table and for the first time she noticed the paperwork spread across it.

"What is all of this?"

He picked up a thick, legal document and handed it to her. Several multicolored Post-it notes stuck out from the pages. "You don't own part of the company."

She scanned the documents. Her brother's half of the company was outlined...his signature was across the bottom. "I don't know what any of this means."

"Nathan sold his half of the company... Well, sort of."

She blinked. What? "But, I have the documents from his lawyer..."

"Which were drafted along with his will a long time ago." He picked up the papers and pointed to the date on the signature line. Two days before the accident. "I found these in his office, and just had time to review them last night."

"You didn't know he was planning to do this?" She frowned.

Ben sat and sighed. "We'd talked about it a few months ago when a third party had expressed interest in becoming a partner, but I didn't know he'd been really considering it. He'd left me a voice mail the day of the…" He paused. "He said he needed to talk to me about something and that he and Rachel were on their way to Newark."

Then the accident happened and they'd never made it.

"I guess this was what he wanted to tell me."

Lindsay stared at the documents, struggling to wrap her mind around what was happening. "So, then I have no control of this community center deal?"

He nodded.

She tossed the papers onto the table. "Well, forget it. I don't want to sell half of the company."

"Nathan already made this decision. And think about it Lindsay—it's the best option for you, too. Once this paperwork gets officially filled, you will have a quarter of a million dollars to invest for the kids' futures."

"But it means I can't stop this community center deal." Her shoulders sagged. She couldn't believe this was happening.

"I already did," he said quietly.

Her head shot up. "You did?"

"Yes. Last night, I emailed the investor and I have a meeting with Mayor Parsons this morning to let him know we are no longer interested."

She blinked.

"So, the community center is safe?"

He nodded. "From Harper Walker Developments, anyway." He stood and, going to the coffeemaker, he poured her a cup. Handing it to her, he said, "Someone else may want to take advantage of a million-dollar development investment deal." He winced. "But not me...not today."

Setting the coffee aside, she stood and hugged him. "Thank you, Ben."

He squeezed her quickly before releasing her. "And there's something else."

She waited.

"I'm heading back to Newark tomorrow."

"You're leaving?" She knew he had to eventually, but they hadn't discussed a definite timeline.

"I think I should. We both know this situation might be convenient but it's not a permanent one and I think it's getting confusing for the kids." His cheeks flushed slightly as he said, "Caleb asked last night if I was going to marry you."

Lindsay choked on a mouthful of coffee. "He did?" She hadn't really given much thought to what the kids must have been thinking, but obviously they'd come to their own conclusions. "What did you tell him?"

"I told him you and I were friends and we didn't need to be married or to live together for me to be a part of their lives." He paused. "And I do want to be a part of their lives. I know you may think I was only here for this deal, but that wasn't the reason. We will figure this out. I'm always here for you and the kids."

She nodded, still in disbelief over everything that had just happened in the last few days. She released a deep breath and with it a month's worth of worry and tension.

Nathan had sold his half of the business for enough money to ease her worry about the future. And she didn't have to worry about the community center anymore. Her thoughts shifted to Noah. She wouldn't have to disappoint him.

"Okay," she said, standing. "Let's go wake the kids."

"HEY, I HEARD about Dominic. Tough break, huh?" Brandon said as he joined Noah, who had already been at the club training for an hour.

The past twenty-four hours had been such a roller coaster of emotions, he couldn't even begin to think clearly about what was next. So, he was running and allowing the competing thoughts to battle among themselves. No matter what else happened, he still had a fight to prepare for.

He slowed the treadmill and reached for his towel to wipe his forehead. "Yeah, he's in pretty bad shape."

"And his own cousin?" Brandon shook his head. "Guess the family isn't planning to press charges?"

"Nope." Whether it was a twisted sense of family loyalty or fear of repercussion, he wasn't sure, but it had been the same way when he'd been growing up on the streets. You took what was coming and moved on.

"I guess he's looking forward to starting college in a few months."

Noah stopped the treadmill. "Unfortunately unless we can figure something out, it doesn't look like he can afford to go." Every time he thought about Dominic's father and his refusal to help his son, his blood boiled.

"That sucks." Brandon paused and glanced around the gym. "You know, we could always use some extra hands around here…if Dominic is interested."

Noah nodded eagerly. "Yeah—I bet he would. I mean, until his ribs heal, he'd have to be on light duty—folding towels and putting away light equipment and stuff—but he'd show up." That he knew for sure. Given any chance to succeed, he knew the boy would step up to the responsibility.

"That's no problem," Brandon said. "Tell him to stop by once he's out of the hospital. Maybe if his cousin and his friends see him hanging out here, they'll leave him alone.

And I'll ask a few of the guys to keep an eye on him."

"Thanks, Brandon. I appreciate it." Noah felt some of the stress slip away as he wrapped his hands for training.

"Oh, and great news about the center."

He stopped. "What about the center?"

"There was an announcement in the Brookhollow View this morning—they've decided not to tear it down."

CHAPTER SIXTEEN

"So, I'll be back next weekend and then the following weekend the kids can come to Newark," Ben said, putting his bag into the back of his Land Rover.

"Okay," Lindsay said, fighting an odd sense of disappointment. He'd been such a great help, but she knew it wasn't fair to keep living together and relying on his support when nothing romantic would ever develop between them.

The night before they'd organized visits for the next six months and she was feeling good about the decision.

"Well, I'll go say goodbye to the kids and then that's it, I guess."

"I'll wait out here," Lindsay said, sitting on the front step as he went inside.

She knew the children would miss him, but they needed to move on. While the past few months had worked and they'd been a good team, it had never felt like a family. And the kids deserved a family. A real one. She hoped she could provide that for them.

The memory of Noah's kiss outside the clinic replayed over and over in her mind. She couldn't help but think it ironic that the man she loved, who claimed to love her, was the one who was completely wrong for her, while the man who'd offered to give up his life in Newark for her and the kids wasn't someone she could love that way.

"Seriously, heart, you couldn't cooperate this one time?" she muttered as the door opened behind her.

"Okay, I'm out," Ben said, sitting next to her on the step. "Unless there's anything else you need?"

"No, I think I got it from here."

He stood and, taking her hand, pulled her to her feet. "You're going to do great with these kids, Lindsay. And I'll still be available—anytime—just call, okay?"

She nodded. "Thanks, Ben."

He leaned forward and kissed the top of her head. "You bet."

"'Bye," she said with a wave as she watched him climb into his vehicle.

It was the right thing to do.

She was going to be okay.

They'd all be okay.

NOAH PARKED HIS bike outside the medical clinic later that day. He had to pick up his clearance form before heading out to Newark that evening for the fight weigh-ins and he was desperate to see Lindsay. She'd obviously changed her mind about the community center and he hadn't thought it possible to love her more than he did, but he'd been wrong. She was giving up something important to her family for the sake of the community. He just hoped she was okay with her decision.

Going inside, he saw her behind the desk and smiled when she glanced up.

"Hi," she said, standing and reaching for a file on the cabinet behind her. "I thought we'd see you in here today." She opened the file and handed him the clearance letter. "Here you are. Try to go easy on the leg… if that's possible."

He took the letter and folding it, he tucked

it into his jacket pocket. "Thanks." He cleared his throat, scanning the nearly empty waiting room, before saying, "And thank you for reconsidering the community center deal…"

She shook her head. "It turned out, I didn't really have a say in the first place. Nathan had sold his rights to the company a few days before…" Her voice trailed away.

He frowned. "So, Ben…?"

"Yes."

The front door opened and a woman with two children entered.

Looking past him, Lindsay smiled. "I'll be with you guys in just a sec." Turning back to him, she said, "I have to get back to work…but…uh…good luck with the fight."

Looking at the clearance form in his hand, for the first time he noticed her signature at the bottom. "You signed this."

"Dr. McCarthy gave me signing authority a few months ago in her absence."

Yet, she'd always made him wait for the doctor's signature before.

She was accepting his choices, but she was also making it clear that there was no chance of a future together. She'd obviously come to terms with that…but what about him?

He sighed and hesitated, searching her expression for any sign…of what he wasn't sure. He found nothing. Maybe this really was the one thing they couldn't move past. "Okay, well, thank Ben for me," he said as he turned to leave.

"He left this morning."

"Noah, I hope you have better aim out there."

Brandon was agitated as Noah's gloved hand slid past the target not for the first time since arriving in the Newark stadium for his UFC debut fight.

"Sorry…try again," Noah mumbled.

Brandon let the pads fall to his sides. "What is it? Is it the pay-per-view thing? Millions of at-home viewers freaking you out?"

Sweat formed at the base of Noah's spine. "Not until now. Thanks a lot." He swung his arms and jogged on the spot, keeping his muscles warm.

His fight was scheduled to start in fifteen minutes, but he couldn't focus. The weigh-in and the prefight conference the evening before had been fine. No injured opponents throwing a curveball into his fight game plan. He'd received a clean bill of health and had even come in a pound under his required weight. But something felt off.

He wasn't looking forward to his UFC debut the way he thought he would. He wasn't feeling the prefight adrenaline or the eagerness to step inside the octagon.

"You're not chickening out, are you?" Dominic asked from the bench.

"No. And don't make me regret getting you this job," he grumbled.

He couldn't get Lindsay out of his mind. He was the right man for Lindsay, he had no doubt. He would be there for her and the kids, love them unconditionally. If only she could trust him enough to—

"Look at me," Brandon said, taking him by the shoulders. "You're ready for this fight. You trained for this. You wanted this. You *have* this. But I need you to focus, because that guy out there wants this win as bad as you do and he'll stop at nothing to get it."

Stop at nothing… Had he tried everything with Lindsay?

He stared at his coach, then around the warm-up room. The warm-up room at the back of a sold-out stadium full of UFC fans. Brandon's grip tightened on his shoulders.

Noah stepped forward to hug his coach quickly.

The official in the corner looked over at them.

He stepped away from Brandon and rotated his shoulders and neck. "Punch me," he said quietly.

Brandon shook his head, his shoulders slumping forward, his hands on his hips. "You're serious? You'd give all of this up—everything we've worked for—for Lindsay?"

"Maybe someday you'll know what it feels like to love—"

The next thing he knew he was flying backward from the hardest left hook he'd ever asked for.

LINDSAY SCANNED THE mess of her home once the kids were tucked into bed. All of her furniture had been wrapped in plastic and moved to the center of the living room in preparation for the furniture arriving from the B and B. "My house will never be the same again," she said into the phone cradled against her shoulder.

"But somehow you sound okay with that," Lily said on the other end.

Lindsay smiled. "I am." Rachel and Nathan's furniture may not have been to her taste, but it was family friendly, life friendly.

"When does Luke arrive with the furniture?"

"Any minute," she said, going to the window and pulling back the curtain.

"Are you going to watch PPV tonight?"

Lindsay glanced at her television screen where the eighty-dollar pay-per-view fights were paused. "Of course not," she said.

Watching them with a hand covering her eyes wasn't really watching, was it?

"You're such a bad liar," Lily said.

The sound of a truck pulling into the yard caught her attention. "Lily, Luke's here. I have to go."

"Call me later. Let me know if he wins."

"Will do," she said, disconnecting the call

and tossing her phone onto her hall table as she opened the door.

"Hey, Lindsay. Should I start bringing stuff in?" Luke asked, opening the tailgate of the truck.

"Yeah, I've made a path," she said, tying her hair back quickly and rolling up her sleeves to help.

Once they'd carried in the sofa and love seat and new end tables, they removed her white furniture. "Harper would have this stuff destroyed in about three minutes," Luke said with the smile of a proud papa.

"She's beautiful, Luke. Not that there was any doubt with you and Vic as parents," she said.

He laughed. "Thanks! I thought you were going to actually let me leave without flirting with me."

She blushed. For once that hadn't been her intent with this man. "Uh, um…"

"Lindsay, I was kidding," he said with a wink.

"Well, that's a huge relief!"

She laughed.

"So, when is the B and B reopening?"

"In a couple of days. Heather has agreed to work the desk during the day and my mom and Mrs. Mason offered to help out in the evenings."

"A family affair."

"Yeah, we'll see how it goes… I swear, some days, I wish those two still weren't talking to each other. Life was simpler back then. Now they compete over showering Harper with gifts and attention."

"Tell them I have five kids here they can shower with gifts and attention anytime," she said.

Luke touched her shoulder. "You're doing good, Lindsay. And our door is always open to you and the kids…just like it always was."

So he remembered the days from their childhood when his family seemed to have everything together and she and Nathan could only find brief respite with them from their mother's emotional turmoil. Not trusting herself to speak, she nodded.

"Okay, I'll take this stuff to Kayla's." His youngest sister had bought all of her furniture a few days before.

"Thanks, Luke."

He climbed back into his truck and drove away with the last remaining evidence of her single life.

THE TATTOO SHOP'S neon sign flashing caught his eye as Noah sped toward the highway. Ten minutes earlier, when the sun was still cresting the horizon, he may not have noticed it, but now it was like a beacon. He slowed the motorcycle slightly. He was desperate to get back to Brookhollow, to Lindsay...but in case his walking away from fighting wasn't enough proof of his commitment and love...

He pulled the bike into the lot and, cutting the engine, he removed his helmet and went inside. A small part of him hoped they didn't take walk-ins...mostly the side of his jaw that was already causing him pain. Brandon hadn't messed around with that punch.

"Can I help you?" A young girl asked, glancing up from a tattoo sketch on the desk in front of her. Her long, bright red hair, shaved on one side to reveal a head tattoo suited her. As did the tattoo sleeves from shoulder to wrist.

"I was wondering if you took walk-ins?"

"Not usually, but there was a cancellation an hour ago... Sit, and I'll go check with Skull."

Skull? "Yeah...sure...okay," Noah said, as she disappeared toward the back of the shop through a swinging door.

The sound of a tattoo gun made him wince. He wasn't afraid of much, but needles...ones that repeatedly pierced the skin...and made that noise... His heart rate increased and he glanced outside toward his bike. He could leave before Skull got his hands on him.

"Hey," a man's voice said behind him.

Too late. He turned and almost laughed in relief. Skull was hardly what he'd been expecting. Five two maybe and a hundred pounds, he looked like that lead singer... the skater-dude from Fall Out Boy. His head-to-toe tattoos and the large ear loops in his ears gave him credibility as a tattoo artist however and Noah relaxed a little. "Hi. I was wondering about getting a tattoo," he said.

"What did you have in mind?" the guy

asked, reaching for a binder behind the counter.

"Honestly, I don't really know...I decided to do this three minutes ago." He had an idea of what he wanted, but the lifelong commitment of such a gesture made his pulse soar...but in a good way.

"Have you been drinking?"

He shook his head. "No. I'm an MMA... was an MMA fighter."

Was.

"Wouldn't have guessed," the guy said sarcastically, and the receptionist laughed.

"What about names? Can you do those?"

The guy shot a look at the redhead. "Yes..." He said slowly. "But...you just admitted to giving this tattoo no thought whatsoever...and now you want a name? You need to be sure about this. Are you?"

"A hundred percent."

LINDSAY HAD FINALLY gotten both babies to sleep when the doorbell rang. If that was Scouts selling those chocolate-covered almonds again, she was going to lose it.

Just in case, she grabbed her wallet on the way to the door.

Swinging it open, her eyes widened.

Noah.

"The fights are over already?" she asked.

They were still paused on her television, as she hadn't been able to bring herself to watch any more. Her eyes surveyed the large bruise and slight swelling on the side of his cheek. She was relieved to see it seemed to be the extent of his injuries.

"Mine is," he said softly.

"Well, you know where the clinic is."

She went to shut the door but he held it open.

"I didn't fight."

She paused to study him.

"Tell that to your face," she said, cocking her head to the side.

"Brandon did this," he said with a wide smile. "Who knew the guy was that good a shot? I thought he was coaching because he was such a lousy fighter." He laughed and touched his bruise, then winced.

Lindsay stared at him in disbelief. "Why would Brandon punch you?"

"To get out of paying the penalties for me bailing on the biggest MMA organization in the world."

He stepped forward. "I quit fighting."

Her heart pounded in her ears. "Noah, it's late. I just put the kids to bed and now I have to sit down and figure out where we all go from here, so I'm going to say goodnight before this gets complicated."

"I'd say we're too late for that." He pushed the door open and stepped inside, wrapping his arms around her. "The thing is…I love you and I'm sorry it took me so long to figure out what I had to do to make you believe that."

"Noah, you can't walk away from fighting for good. You love it."

"Not as much as I love you," he said.

She swallowed hard, desperately wanting to believe him. "It's your career."

"Ethan offered me a full-time job at the fire hall. I'm going to take it."

"But that's not your dream. You won't be happy." If he gave up fighting, he would only resent her in time.

"Being with you…and these kids…will make me happy."

She sighed. "And that's it? No more fighting?"

"No more fighting."

She still hesitated.

Reaching into his pocket, he took out his phone and handed it to her. "Read the text message from the fight match-maker for the organization."

Lindsay scrolled through the messages to the one he meant and her heart stopped. "You're done fighting MMA."

She handed him back his phone.

"Noah, I can't believe you did this."

"Make it worthwhile. Tell me you'll finally give me…give *us* a chance now."

She looked around her home, littered with toys. "I come as a package deal of six."

"I'll take it… Maybe we can become eight or nine…" He kissed her cheeks and her nose. "So, is that a yes? You'll give me a chance now that I'm running toward burning buildings instead of fighting?"

She kissed him quickly. "That's heroic,

not stupid. Besides, there's a fire in Brook-hollow once every twenty years."

He pulled her closer and rested his forehead against hers. "What about the one that's been burning between us? What do we do about that one?"

Her gaze met his and her heart swelled with love for the man who'd put a future with her above everything else.

"Let it burn," she whispered, standing on tiptoe and steadying herself against his chest as she kissed him. A soft, slow, torturous kiss as she gave herself over completely to him.

He'd given up fighting for her. For a future together. She'd never asked and he'd done it anyway.

"Oh, there is one more thing," he said, taking a step back and pulling up the sleeve of his leather jacket.

She gasped at the sight of her name in black ink across his forearm. "Tell me that's not real."

"It better be after I braved all of those tiny, painful needles," he said.

She gently touched the swollen, red skin

around the tattoo then punched his shoulder. "I can't believe you did this." Just when she thought his recklessness was a thing of the not-too-distant past.

"I thought you'd like it."

"You're crazy," she said, the corners of her mouth betraying her with a smile.

She loved it. She loved the gesture. She loved him.

"Maybe." He pulled her close again, tucking a stray strand of hair behind her ear.

"I mean, what if I didn't love you?" she teased.

"That didn't stop me from loving you before."

She swallowed a lump in the back of her throat. "I do love you…despite my best efforts and common sense. I love you, Noah."

"That's great news, because my other option was to date women named Lindsay from now on," he said against her lips, a mischievous gleam in his eyes.

"Shut up and kiss me again." She pulled him closer, but he resisted.

"Just a sec." He bent, removed his shoes and placed them on the rack next to the door, next to her shoes and five sets of little ones. "Better," he said, wrapping his arms around her once more.

"Better," she whispered as his lips met hers.

* * * * *